THE SONG OF MANIK CHANDRA

THE SONG OF MANIK CHANDRA

GEORGE A. GRIERSON

GYAN

Published by

GYAN

Gyan Publishing House
5, Ansari Road
Daryaganj, New Delhi-110002
Phone: 011-47034999, 9811692060
E-mail: books@gyanbooks.com

Distribution Network
gyanbooks.com
India, USA, Canada, UK, Australia

ISBN: 978-93-7097-735-8 (PB)

First Published, 1878

2nd Impression 2025

Printed at: Gyan Press, Delhi.

THE SONG OF MANIK CHANDRA
Author: GEORGE A. GRIERSON

THE

SONG OF MÁNIK CHANDRA.

BY

G. A. GRIERSON, C. S.

1878.

THE SONG OF MANIK CHANDRA,

BY

G. A. GRIERSON, C. S.

Introduction.

In my notes on the Rangpur dialect, I promised to give an account of the song whose name heads this article, and that promise I shall now do my best to redeem. I find, however, that the task has been more difficult than I anticipated. I do not doubt but that king Mánik Chandra, and his terrible wife did once exist; but the traditions current concerning him run so counter to ascertained history, that I have been able to discover very few grains of truth amongst the legendary chaff that has accumulated about his name.

To begin with; the first name we meet with is a crux. Mánik Chandra's brother was a *Pála* king.

Mánik Chandra himself was certainly not a *Pála*, for he was a *baniyá* by caste, while Abul-Fazl describes the *Pálas* as *Kayasthas.** Moreover, I know of no dynasty of *Pála* kings, containing names ending in "Chandra," like Mánik Chandra, Gopí Chandra, or Bhava-Chandra. The brother's name was Dharma Pál.

The following account has been drawn from various sources. I have consulted BUCHANAN throughout, and wherever his story differs from mine in important particulars I have recorded the points of disagreement.

* Cf. however, Mr. Westmacott's article on the *Pál* Kings, in Vol. LIX of the *Calcutta Review*, on which I have drawn freely, and gratefully, while treating on the present subject.

In the *Ḍimlá Ṭháná* situated to the north-west of Rangpur, and nine or ten miles to the south-east of the sub-divisional head quarters of *Bágḍokará* is the city of Dharma Pál. Buchanan thus describes it—"It is in the form of a parallelogram, rather less than a mile from north to south, and half a mile from east to west. The following sketch (Fig. 1) taken in riding round it, will enable the reader more easily to understand it than my account.* The defences consist of a high rampart of earth, which at the south-east corner is irregular, and retires back to leave a space that is much elevated, and is said to have been the house of the Rájá's minister *(Díván-khána)*. On the east side I observed no traces of a ditch, nor gate; but a ditch about 40 feet wide surrounds the other three faces.† In the centre of each of these is a gate defended by outworks, and in these are a good many bricks. At each angle of the fort has been a small square projection, like a sort of bastion, extending however only across the counter-scarp to the ditch; and between each gate and the bastion at the corner are some others of similar construction. The earth from the ditch has been thrown outwards, and forms a slope without a covered way. At the distance of about 150 yards from the ditch of the north-east and south sides, are parallel ramparts and ditches, which enclose an outer city, where it is said the lower populace resided. Beyond these on the south is another enclosure, in which it is said the horses were kept. Parallel to the west side of the city, at about the distance of 150 yards, runs a fine road very much raised; but its ends have been swept away by changes that have taken place in the rivers."

To the west of this city at a distance of two miles, was the city of Mánik Chandra, now, however, called, after his more famous wife *Mayaná Matir koṭ*.‡

Here Mánik Chandra reigned over the half dozen square miles of territory which constituted him a *rájádhirája*. His wife Mayaná was deeply skilled in magic, an art which it appears in those days, though unlawful for a man, was lawful for a woman.§ She was (so says the legend) the pupil of a mighty magician who by his intense devotion to and abstraction into the Holy Name had acquired immense powers. His mere word was sufficient to strike one dead. He could cause the sea to cease to move,

* The plan given is Buchanan's, and is very fairly accurate. The city is noted for containing within the inner walls three remarkably fine tanks.

† The ditch and rampart are called in Rangpur the *Koṭ* (कोट अर्थात् बड स्थान व्यापिया मृत्तिकार उच्च एकटा गड़) G. A. G.

‡ मयना मतिर कोट. This lady is said to have founded several other important towns. Amongst names which still survive I may mention *Mayaná talir háṭ* (मयना तलीर हाट) and *Mayaná Guḍí* (मयना गुड़ी)

§ See verse 60 of the poem.

and the lights in his dwelling burnt with surpassing splendour, though only fed with Ganges water.

Now this man was a sweeper.

The Ha'di Siddha.

He was a *Háḍi*, the caste which acts as sweeper in Bangál. In Rangpur its impurity signifies nameless abomination, a fact which should be specially noted. Rangpur forms part of Kámarúpa. Hither one of the five *Paṇḍavas* never set his foot, and the land is consequently impure. Its men are not as other men, nor its laws as other laws. It has a special code of its own, most of which can be found in the *Yoginí Tantra;* and this law allows many things (such as certain kinds of flesh eating) to its straitest sects of Bráhmaṇs. Hence impurity in Western India frequently becomes purity in Rangpur; while Rangpur impurity includes things simply inconceivable in *Arya varta.*

The Háḍi of the poem, and of the popular legends of the present day was a *Vaishṇava;* and as Mayaná was also of the same sect (in which the members are practically all of one caste) it is not impossible that she should have had such a man for her Guru.

I say only "not impossible," for I consider it highly improbable, and for the following reasons :—It is evident that the true story has been much transformed in its passage from mouth to mouth, and I believe that the principle recasting (if I may call it so) was due to the influence of the *Vaishṇava* followers of Chaitanya. Translated into common English the story is that Mayaná's chaplain was a man of remarkable sanctity, whom the populace credited with supernatural powers. He was a great saint, and his religion followed that of his historians. The *Yogís* who narrate his history are at the present day followers of the teachers of the religion of Vishṇu (not, be it observed, the popular *Vaishṇavas, vulgo Boishṭoms);* and they naturally claimed their hero as belonging to their own sect. It is peculiarly the tendency of this beautiful, almost Christian, religion to preach the doctrine of the equality of castes ;—how every valley shall be exalted, and the rough places made smooth. The lowest amongst the low,—the despised and rejected amongst men, is fully capable of attaining equal holiness with the strictest Bráhmaṇ of the holiest sect which worships at the shrines of *Vṛindávana.* Such being the case, what is more natural than that the ignorant and illiterate members of the same religion, who (like the *Yogís)* have the traditions of a missionary priesthood in their family, should instinctively point out how even an abominable Háḍi can attain the terrible powers which their fathers attributed to a *Vaśishṭha* or to a *Durvása.*

But, now that I have shown that it is quite possible for such an idea to have arisen, I would point out that the man who is now called the

Háḍi Siddha cannot have been originally a *Vaishṇava* at all, and was never by caste a Háḍi. He is still occasionally addressed as Haripa (not Háḍipa, or Háripa), which is quite a possible name for a follower of Hari; but on going back even so short a space as the first decade of the present century, we find that Dr. Buchanan, whose powers of observation are unquestioned, describes the Guru of Mayaná Mati as a *Yogí* by caste, whose name was Haripa while he never once mentions the fact of his being Háḍi, which is now much the commoner name. Now in the Rangpur dialect, *a* is frequently lengthened, and *r* is interchangeable with *ḍ* so that the change from *Hari* to *Haḍi* is easy, and such a change, having once taken common currency, would have itself suggested the idea so peculiarly *Vaishṇava* to which I have before alluded. (Cf. Max Muller's lectures on the science of language, for evidence as to the tendency of false etymology and of phonetic decay in originating popular legends.) This Haripa, according to Buchanan was the pupil of Kanipa,* who was the pupil of Gorakshanáth. Ṭhání Ḍimlá, where these *Yogís* live, is close to Nipál, and we must go there to find out who Gorakshanáth is. I am now writing in Supaul, in the north of Bhágulpur, and not twenty miles from the Nipál frontier; and what I have heard about him here, confirms in a remarkable degree what Buchanan tells of him. The dwellers of the low lands will have nought of him, and we do not find his *cultus* till we reach the half savage Buddhist dwellers of the interior. Here we discover a curious mixture of the *Mahá Bhárata* and Buddhism. They say that during Yudhishṭhira's journey through the pathless tracts of the Himálaya to heaven, his brethren (as we know) fell behind, one by one, and perished miserably. Here, adds the Nipálí, only one survived,—the club-bearing Bhíma. He was saved by a Buddhist saint called Gorakshanáth who after performing many wondrous acts made him king over Nipál.†

* I know of no religious teacher called Kanipa. There was a Kanapa, who was a teacher of the Ja*m*gama sect of the S'aivas, (Mackenzie *apud* Wilson I. 227), who was of some celebrity, and it is just possible that his name may have been adopted by the Yogís, who were originally a S'aiva caste.

† The above is the popular tradition I have gathered from oral accounts. The following summary of what is noticeable about Gorakshanáth and the Yogís is gathered principally from Wilson.

The first teacher of Buddhism in Nipál, was Manju, who came from Maháchín and who made the valley of Khatmáṇḍu, formerly a lake, habitable by cutting through the mountains with his scymitar. He taught a pure form of Buddhism, which became afterwards impregnated with Bráhmaṇical ideas through the invitation given by Narendra Deva, king of Nipál, to one Matsyendra Náth a teacher of the *Pásupata* form of the S'aiva religion. This was apparently about the 7th century A. D. This Matsyendra was in reality the Lokes'vara Padmapáṇi, who descended to the earth by command of the Ádi Buddha, and hid himself in the belly of a fish, in order to overhear S'íva teach Párvatí the doctrine of the *Yoga*, and Wilson shows that Padmapáṇi came either from the east or from the north of Bangál.

It is quite natural that the Buddhists should claim him as their saint, but in reality he was nothing of the sort. He was a teacher of the *S'aiva* religion, and one of the reputed founders of the sect of *Yogís*. Whether the *Yogís* of Rangpur are an off-shoot of the Nipálí converts, or whether Gorakshanáth and his fellows came from north-eastern Bangál, or from A'sám,. where the *Páśupata cultus*, whose followers finally became *Yogís*, was established I cannot pretend to decide. I am inclined to believe in the former hypothesis, for they themselves have a tradition, that *they came from the west*, having formerly been pupils of S'ankaráchárya, who were expelled by him for indulging in spirituous liquor. Besides, they reject, to the present day, the authority of Bráhmaṇs, and have their own priests; and this is just what would be expected from people coming from Buddhistic Nipál. They rose too to power under a dynasty of Pálas, most of the members of which family were Buddhists. Be that as it may, this much however is certain, that at the time of Mánik Chandra, the Yogís practised a *S'aiva* religion and worshipped a deified teacher of their sect, also worshipped in Nipál, named Gorakshanáth. Gorakshanáth moreover, had already supplanted S'iva himself, and was alone worshipped by his followers.

The poem annexed bears abundant witness to this. At every *Nodus* whether *Vindice dignus* or not, he is brought in as a *deus ex machina;*

Sixth in descent from Matsyendra Náth, in the time of spiritual teachers, comes Goraksha Náth, who, according to this, ought to have flourished in the 8th century. There must however be some mistake here, for it is known that Goraksha Náth was a contemporary of Kabír, and held a controversy with him which is extant *(Gorakh Náth ki Goshṭhí*, W. I. 213), and Kabír lived in the 15th century. Hence, unless the list of teachers in the *Haṭha Pradipa* (W. I. 214) is incorrect, Matsyendra Náth must have lived at a much later period than that tentatively assigned to him by Wilson. Another Narendra Deva reigned in Nipál in the 12th century, and it is possible that it is he who introduced Matsyendra Náth, in which case the discrepancy would not be so outrageous. But, here another difficulty arises, we find that we must date Goraksha Náth's pupils' pupil as flourishing in the 14th century, a fact which agrees better with the theory of Narendra Deva II; but then, what becomes of Kabír?

We have seen that Matsyendra Náth taught *Páśupata S'aivism*, and it is a well known fact that the *Káṇphâṭá Yogís*, to which sect those who sing the *Mánik Chandra* song belong, are the representatives at the present day of that form of religion. The above account in no way tallies with the tradition mentioned later on, in the text, that the *Yogís* were errant pupils of S'ankaráchárya, nor is such a story borne out by the *S'ankara Vijaya*. In chapter 41, S'ankara successfully combats the *Yoga* doctrine, but he treats his opponents with a respect which he would never extend to backsliding disciples (S. V. c. 41. Bibl. Indica, Ed. p. 198).

That the Yogís rapidly became an important sect is evident from the numerous temples dedicated to Goraksha Náth, not only in Nipál but in the Panjáb and North West Provinces. We read that the Emperor Akbar consorted with them. He was initiated into their learning, and, on one occasion, ate with them, at one of their festivals.

not as an ordinary saint, but leading the whole Hindú Pantheon, and the characters of the Mahábhárata to boot. It is Gorakshanáth, and not S'iva, who grants a boon, or comforts a sorrowing widow on her husband's funeral pyre. As he is considered in Nipál, so he is here, a saint whose austerities have rendered him not only an omnipotent but The Omnipotent, and who has always been proof against the charms of the most wanton Apsarases ever sent for a holy man's seduction by a terrified *Svarga.* We are bound therefore to assume that the guru of the Lady Mayaná, whatever his name was, and whom for the sake of simplicity we can call the Siddha was a *Yogí, i. e.* a *S'aiva* by religion, and professed doctrines which were professed also by semi-Buddhist races in Nipál.

As this introduction relates to the Mánik Chandra poem, I shall, now that I have stated my opinion concerning his identity, for the future call him as he is called in the modern edition of the poem, the Háḍi Siddha.

Dharma Pa'la.

The Háḍi Siddha was, as I have already said, of great power, but his pupil Mayaná, by dint of continued practice of her magic art, became greater still. She could control everything but fate; and the whole of the poem is nothing but a description of her struggles with that resistless passive energy.

According to universal tradition both in Buchanan's time, and at the present day, her husband, Mánik Chandra was brother of Dharma Pála. This I have before shown, is an impossibility if the names are correct.

In order to obtain an approximate date for Dharma Pála it is necessary to consider two lists of dynasties. They are now-a-days the traditional history, and they agree with Buchanan's account. The following are those I have collected:

1. Dharma Pála.
2. Mánik Chandra (his brother; died early).
3. Gopí Chandra.
4. Bhava Chandra.
5. A Pála Rájá. Name unknown.
6. Here Buchanan reasonably suggests a period of anarchy.
7. Níla Dhvaja.
9. Chakra Dhvaja.
10. Nílámbara.

According to Buchanan, Nílámbara was defeated by Husain Sháh about the year 1500 A. D.; and thus, allowing six reigns to a century, (a moderate estimate), we must date Dharma Pál as having flourished about the year 1350 A. D.; he certainly (if he ever existed, and if the dynasty lists are true) cannot have lived much before the commencement of the 14th century, *i. e.*, before our English King Edward III.

Abul-Fazl gives a list of ten Pála Kings quoted by Mr. Westmacott; and they became extinct about the middle of the eleventh century thus leaving a space of 250 years to be accounted for. Hence it need not necessarily be determined that Dharma Rájá was a member of the great family of Pála Kings. Buchanan suggests that he may have represented the remains of a family which survived the wreck of the dynasty, to save a portion of the kingdom which remained unconquered, by the successors of Ádi Súra in Rangpur; and the fact is not rendered less improbable when we consider the history of the Háḍi Siddha. We know that the Pála kings were, when we first meet them, Buddhists and that subsequently some branches of the family changed their religion to some one or other of the many varying sects of Hindúism. If then Dharma Pála ruled in a country in which such a holy man was arch-priest, it is rather a confirmation than otherwise of this theory. I myself think it certain that Dharma Pála was a member, or descendant of the great Pála family, for Dr. Buchanan gives an illustration of an image found in his city, which contains the typical Pála emblem of an elephant borne down by a lion. (Fig. 2.)

We thus I think can be certain of the following facts,—that early in the 14th century a king named Dharma Pála ruled over a small tract of country near the Karatoyá river in the present districts of Rangpur and Jalpaiguri. That this Dharma Pála was a member of the great Pála family which once ruled over northern Ba*m*ga. That in his territory there was a saint of considerable sanctity, then living, who professed tenets borrowed possibly from Nipál. And that close to his capital city there lived in a fortified stronghold a powerful chief named Mánik Chandra, who was married to a lady called Mayaná. It may be gathered from local tradition that Mayaná was an ambitious and designing woman, and that she acknowledged the saint above-named as her spiritual instructor.

Between the king and the chief, according to local tradition, a war arose, which ended in the defeat and disappearance of the former, and triumph of the latter, in a great battle fought on the banks of the river Hángrigosha. The battle-field is still shown, a mile or so to the north of Dharmapur.

Ma'nik Chandra.

After this victory, Mánik Chandra took up his residence at Dharmapur, while the Lady Mayaná remained at her old home ***Mayaná Matir kot*** probably to be near her old Guru, the ruins of whose home are still shown in the neighbourhood.

The further particulars regarding Mánik Chandra will be gathered from the annexed poem. Who he was we cannot tell, we must be content with knowing that he was a neighbouring chief of Dharma Pála and his conqueror.

He appears to have governed at first with vigour and success. We read of rustic wealth and security, and light taxation. The revenue system is worth noticing, it was a peculiarly elastic and simple land tax.* The land in those days was little more than a wild forest, and the soil poor and barely cultivated. The sparse *prajás* scraped with their flimsy ploughs the surface of the sandy soil immediately round their homestead and struggled lazily for bare existence. I suspect that, even in king Mánik's time, life and property were not over secure, and under these circumstances it was necessary that the taxes should be light. Each plough-owner was therefore required to pay for each plough in his homestead thirty *káoṛís* per mensem.† Under the light taxation which may be inferred from this absurd exaggeration of the text, the *prajás* were necessarily happy and contented, until Mánik Chandra did what was in Rangpur the most unpopular thing a zamíndár could do. He engaged a Bangálí Díván. I have in my previous paper enlarged on the hatred of the Rangpurí peasantry for a genuine freshly imported native of the south, and I need not dwell upon it here. Suffice it to say that the new Díván fully bore out the character of his nation, for he immediately doubled the land-tax. The result was a rising of the peasants, and according to their account, the mysterious death of the king shortly afterwards from the effects of Rangpur fever. He left no living child, but his wife Mayaná was subsequently confined of a posthumous one. The child was not born till eighteen months after Mánik's death,—and ill-natured people might feel inclined to consider Mánik Chandra's claim to the title of father not proved ; but the poem chivalrously comes to the rescue of Mayaná's reputation, and makes her pass through a long series of puerile adventures (the old tale of Orpheus and Eurydiké with the characters reversed), and finally obtain from Gorakshanáth, and his attendant gods, the boon of having a son of such perfect vigour and

* The same system prevails to the present day in parts of Nipál, where the demand for land is not so great as it is in the more settled British territory. A plough is there, however, only considered as equivalent to eight bigas, the average rent for a plough of land being considerably below that current on this side of the frontier.

† The text says $1\frac{1}{2}$ *buḍis* of *káoris*. A *buḍi* is five *gandas* or twenty. One *buḍi* of *káoris* = a pice. $1\frac{1}{2}$ pice a month = 4 ánás, 6 pie, per year per plough. In the light soil of Rangpur, one plough can easily cultivate fifteen *bigas* or five acres of land, so that the annual land-tax was, according to the text, less than $3\frac{3}{5}$ pies per *biga*, or than a penny farthing per acre.

virtue that it would take at least twenty-five months to fashion him. As a matter of special grace he was presented to her with seven months of his growth already accomplished, so that he was in fact born only eighteen months after his conception.*

During Mayaná's pregnancy she became *satí* for her dead husband, and mounted the pyre with his corpse. I need hardly say that the flames refused to touch her, although the relations of her late husband did their best to aid them, by thrusting her more and more into the flames with long poles.†

Mayaná after passing through various adventures survives them all, and in due time gives birth to a son, who is called Gopí Chandra. It is he who is really the hero of the poem, and not his putative father who gives it his name. All references to the latter end before the 154th verse, and the remaining 550 narrate the fortunes of his son.

Apparently from the birth of her child, Mayaná deserted Mayaná matír koṭ and went to dwell in Dharmapur. She was a clever woman and managed to keep up without great difficulty the high rates of land revenue, which had caused the death of her husband.‡ When Gopí Chandra was nine years old, it was time for him to be married, and so Mayaná looked round for a suitable match.

Ra'ja' Hari's' Chandra.

At the present day, seven or eight miles south of the ruins of Dharmapur, in the ṭháná of Darváni, there is a village called Char Chará.§ Here there is a large mound of earth called Haríś Chandra Rájár Páṭ, *i. e.*, the seat of king Haríś Chandra.

Buchanan described it as a circular mound of earth about 40 feet in diameter. "In searching for materials to build a pig-stye, the heap was opened by an indigo-planter, and a building of stones was discovered. The

* The Yogís of course see nothing extraordinary in this ludicrous idea. They say the events occurred in the *Satya Yuga*, when all things were possible. I asked a Yogí once why the child was presented to Mayaná already seven months developed, and he explained that it was "to prevent excessive scandal," which might have occurred if the child had been born twenty-five months after his father's death!! This is straining at a gnat, and swallowing a camel with a vengeance.

† The description of this rite in the poem is curious enough: whether such conduct on the part of the relations was common in the performance of it I do not know. I have been unable to identify Chánd the merchant, who figures in this part of the poem with any other legend.

‡ I gather this from the last verse of the poem, from which it is evident that it was not till Gopí Chandra's return that the land revenue was reduced to its former level.

§ चर चरा, it is a short distance due east of the better known रामगञ्ज टुपामारि *Rámganj Ṭupámári.*

upper parts of this, consisting of many long stones, were removed, when a friend of more science in antiquities, recommended the planter to abstain from further depredations. In its present state the lower part only of the building remains and is a cavity of about 13 feet square at the mouth, and 8 at the bottom. The sides are lined with squared stones, which form a deep stair on each side, and the walls are exceedingly thick. My description will be more easily understood by consulting the plan (fig. 3). I have no doubt that this is a tomb."

Since Buchanan's time it has been still further desecrated, and, now, little remains beyond the mound of earth and the name.

Hariś Chandra had two daughters Aduná and Paduná.* These he gave in marriage to Gopí Chandra with a hundred maid-servants to wait upon them.† By his eighteenth year Gopí Chandra had no child. It had been foretold to Mayaná that at that age he would die unless he became a Sannyásí.‡ So he prepared, much against his will, to go forth wandering in the forests with the Háḍi Siddha. His two wives Aduná and Paduná tried hard to persuade him to stay, and their arguments form, in my opinion, by far the best portion of the poem (vv. 243-302). They contain many touches of true poetry.

This flight of fancy, however, almost immediately leads us into the most unnatural—the profoundest bathos. The king tempted by his wives, in order to put the correctness of his mother's words to the test, makes her pass through the ordeal of boiling oil. Although the king has strength of mind to keep his mother in boiling oil for nine days, it is gratifying to learn that he really was a tender and affectionate son; for when he found at the expiration of that time that his mother had been boiled to death, he began to weep. Mayaná of course was really not dead, she had only changed herself into a grain of mustard seed, and soon reappeared in her proper form. After the usual preparations, the king sets out on his journey with the Háḍi Siddha. His minor adventures need not be recorded here. He passed through many trials as preparations for his future, and finally in an evil moment promised to let the Háḍi have twelve *káoṛís* wherewith to buy *gánjá*. When he would have given it, he found that the store from which he intended to take it had been spirited away. Thereupon, rather

* In Buchanan, Hudna and Pudna.

† Buchanan says that Gopí Chandra had a hundred wives, but I can find no trace of this in any modern legend. The maid-servants may have been concubines, but not wives. They are the hundred damsels mentioned in verse 242. They are it is true called queens in verse 410,—but that is only part of the gross and puerile exaggeration displayed there, Aduná and Paduná being still kept separate.

‡ V. 241. The term Sannyásí should be noticed. It is the ordinary term for a Śaiva mendicant, Vairágí usually representing a Vaishṇava one.

than break his promise, he told his companion to pawn him for the money. The Háḍi took him at his word to the *bázár*, where all the women fell in love with him, which gives rise to an amusing scene. However they could not afford the twelve *káoṛís* demanded ; so the Háḍi finally took him to the house of a harlot named Hírá.

Hi'ra' the Harlot.

According to popular tradition, Hírá is said to have lived at "Kholá Kuṭá a village in the west of the Dinájpur District." This place I have been unable to identify. Mr. Westmacott, who has most kindly taken much trouble in assisting me on this point, suggests that the place may be Kholá Háṭi, a village in the east of that District, where the Dinájpur and Rangpur road crosses the river Karatoyá. There were lately extensive ruins to its north, but they have been excavated by the Northern Bengal Railway people for ballast. This theory is not at all so improbable as it might seem at first sight, for every tradition leads us to believe that Hírá's residence was near the Karatoyá. Dinájpur is to the west of Rangpur, and if the original belief was that Kholá Kuṭá (? Kholá Háṭi) was "to the west in Dinájpur" the change for "in" to "of" need not surprise us. The locality of Hírá's house is not mentioned in the poem, but a reference to v. 658 will show that it probably was Kholá Háṭi.

Hírá, of course, fell in love with the king, and, being a woman of property, easily found it in her power to borrow the twelve *káoṛís* from a neighbouring banker. The banker drew up the deed of transfer, conveying Gopí Chandra to the harlot's sole use and possession for a period of twelve years, and she then and there paid over the money, and took delivery. The procedure of the sale is worth noticing (vv. 537-546).

After obtaining possession of the king, Hírá had him bathed and adorned in gorgeous apparel; she then sent for him and tried to tempt him, but though she exerted all her fascinations, and the king was almost yielding, she failed ignominiously, Gopí Chandra piously remembering his mother's parting words.* Indignant at her repulse the harlot went to the other extreme, and put him to perform the meanest and vilest offices of her household. The king was continually ill-used, and beaten, and one of his hardest daily labours, was carrying twelve *bhángí* loads of water from the Karatoyá to her house.

On the last day of the twelve years he went to draw water as usual,—but his strength failed him and he fell into the river.

* Gopí Chandra is much lauded for his continence, but, as it appears that the Háḍi before leaving him made him a neuter, there is really little ground for credit.

The beginning of the end.

When the king left his home, his two queens retired from the outer world and shut themselves up in a well-guarded palace. The hundred concubines appear to have become the willing property of a foundling called Khetu, whom Mayaná had cherished and brought up together with her son. This man had subsequently entered Gopí Chandra's service, in the days of his power.

Aduná and Paduná set themselves to playing dice, for they knew that as long as lucky numbers were thrown, the king their husband was well.

The dice continued to fall prosperously until the king fell into the Karatoyá, and then they fell in disarray. A parrot and his mate beheld the tears of their mistresses, and consoling them, offered to go in search of Gopí Chandra.

After some days* the birds found their master, and gave the message of his queens. The king, thereupon wrote a letter on the leaf of a wild plant which grew by, and sent it by them to his mother, who on receiving intelligence of her son summoned the Háḍi, who in his turn went to the king.

The Háḍi then proceeds to distribute poetical justice all round. All the woes which Hírá had inflicted upon Gopí Chandra, she is made to suffer herself. He then cut her in two, her upper half becoming a bat, and her lower half a minnow.

The Harlot's maid-servant was cursed to become as her mistress had been, and in her old age to marry a peon, who would beat her every day of her life. Finally we have the fruit of all the king's penance in his being imbued with a knowledge of the magic art by his eating a filthy mess of the Háḍi's concoction, and he returns home, still however wearing his pilgrim's weeds. His maid-servant was the first to see him, but she did not recognize him. His own wives wavered in their recognition when he denied his identity. The only being that did not hesitate, was his faithful elephant who made obeisance to him while he was yet afar off.

After the usual festivities Gopí Chandra again ascended the throne, and made his subjects happy by fixing the land revenue again at the old rate of thirty *káoṛís*.

Concluding remarks.

Such is the epic of Rangpur, containing here and there a tiny pearl of interest, hidden amidst the rubbish, which is mainly presented to our view. I have ventured to write so much about it, and to submit it to the Society for three reasons.

* There is considerable confusion here amid dates.

First, I believe that men more competent than I, may be able to add a little to the history of the Pála kings, after considering it. Second, because it exhibits a curious, and most instructive lesson as to how a purely S'aiva hero celebrated by men of a S'aiva sect has given rise to a poem of S'aiva foundation, but of Vaishṇava superstructure, and sung by the descendants of these same men. Nay more, how a distinctly S'aiva sect, has become to all intents and purposes a Vaishṇava one, while it still retains its old gods, and its old heroes. It would not be difficult to find parallel transformations in more modern religious history. Thirdly, and more for this reason than any other, because it is a very fair specimen of the peculiar Rangpurí *patois*. And here it may be noticed, that any parts purely and distinctly Vaishṇava interpolations or additions (*e. g.* the introductory lines) are written in a Bengálí much more classical, than the rude language of the S'aiva ground-work. This will be evident to any one who pays attention while reading.

The song is usually sung by four men,—and in parts, not in unison. I am not sufficiently acquainted with Hindu music to give the technical name of the chant. It certainly is the only song I have heard in this country in which harmony is introduced. The top notes of the chant are as follows:

To be sung an octave lower than written.

This is sung chant-like, so as to go once to each line, but leaving the three last notes without words. To these last three notes, the words "He! Rájá!" "He! Mayaná!" "He! Yame!" or some such apostrophe which depends on the person whose adventures are being immediately narrated, are sung as a sort of burden. An example will make this clear. Take the first line of verse six. It is sung thus—

8vo Basso ....

I do not give the harmonies of this, because I cannot. I tried to reproduce them on a harmonium, but though I believe I got the separate notes of each part correctly first on a violin, from the mouth of each singer, when I tried them together I got nothing but a common-place sort of chant, containing one or two consecutive octaves, and not a particle of the spirit of what I had just heard sung. The above is the music of the narrative portion of the poem. Each "*duyá*," has a separate melody of its own.

As the song is sung, the upper part is accompanied in unison on the *saringa*, of which an illustration, taken from Buchanan is appended.

(Fig. 4.) The open note is tuned to E flat

and the higher notes are formed by pressing down the wire on the various projecting knobs over which it passes.

In conclusion, as I stated in my former paper, the poem is in many places unintelligible to every body I have met. In such places *(satya yuger kathás)* the singers have sometimes traditional interpretations. In one or two cases, however, they do not profess even to such: and, I trust, that I may be pardoned under such circumstances for giving a literal translation, without attempting to educe sense out of the arrant nonsense thus arrived at.

मानिक चन्द्र राजार गान।

भाविश्रो रामेर नाम चिन्तिश्रो एक मने।
लइले रामेर नाम कि करिवे यमे॥ १
अधमे ना नैल नाम जीभेर आलिसे।
अम्रतेर भाण्ड तनु गरासिल विषे॥ २
हेंटे याइते ये जन रामेर नाम लय़।
धनुक वान लैया़ राम भक्त सङ्गे याय़॥ ३
राम नामेर नौका खान श्रीगुरु काण्डारी।
दुइ वाऊ पसरिया़ डाके आस पार करि॥ ४
रामेर वन्दन हइल मस्तक उपर।
थुइया़ रामेर गुन सिद्धार गुन गाइ।
याके वन्दिलेइ सिद्धि पाइ॥ ५

मानिक चन्द्र राजा वङ्गे वड़ सति।
हाल खानाय़ मासड़ा साधे देड़ वुड़ि कड़ि॥ ६
देड़ वुड़ी कड़ी लोके खाजना योगाय़।
अष्टमि पुजार दिने पांठा गोटे लय़॥ ७
खड़ीवेचा हैये ये खड़ी भार योगाय़।
तार वदली छय़ मास पाल खाय़॥ ८
पातवेचा हैये ये पात आटि योगाय़।
तारे वदली छय़ मास पाल खाय़॥ ९
एत मानिक चन्द्र राजा सख्या़ नालेर वेड़ा।
एकतन येकतन करे ये खाइके तार दुया़रत घोड़ा।
घिने वान्दि नाहि पिन्दे पाटेर पाछड़ा॥ १०
कारो माड़ाल केह ना याय़
कारो पुष्कनीर जल केह ना खाय़॥ ११

१। यमे। The usual form for Nom. Sing. in Rangpurí. See my "Notes." Most of the irregular grammatical forms contained in this poem will be found therein, and hence I shall not usually draw attention to them here. ॥ २। जीभेर आलिसे = जिह्वेर आलस्ये। गरासिल = ग्रास करिल॥ ४। पसरिया़ = प्रसरिया़। १०। एकतन येकतन = एमन येमन, अर्थात् येमन तेमन। घिने वान्दि = घृणा वान्दिया, अर्थात् घृणा करिया॥

भाटि हइते आइल वाङ्गाल लम्बा लम्बा दाड़ि ।
सेइ वाङ्गाल आसिया मुलुकत् कैल्ल काड़ी ॥ १२
आछिल देड़ वुड़ि खाजना लैल पोनार गण्डा ॥ १३
नाङ्गल वेचाय् जोङ्गाल वेचाय् आरो वेचाय् फाल ।
ख़ाजनार तापते वेचाय् दुधेर छाओयाल ॥ १४
रांड़ी काङ्गाल दुःखिर वड़ दुख्क हइल ।
खाने खाने तालुक सव छन हइया गेल ॥ १५
छोट रायत उठे वले वड़ रायत भाइ ।
प्रधानेर वरावर सवे चल याइ ॥ १६
कि आज्ञा वले प्रधान सकल ।
येत रायत परामस करिया प्रधानेर वाड़ी वैले चैले गेल ॥ १७
केमन वुद्धि करि भाइ केमन समाचार ।
असति राजा हइल राज्येर भितर ॥ १८
प्रधान वले रायत सकल ए वुद्धि नाइ आमार वरावर ।
चल याइ सिवेर वरावर कि आज्ञा वले वोला महेश्वर ॥ १९
यत रायत परामस करिया गेल सिवेर वरावर ॥ २०
सिव ठाकुर वैले तोले छाड़े राओ ।
घरे छिल सिव ठाकुर वाहिरे दिले पाओ ॥ २१
सिवके देखिया रायत जन करे परनाम ।
गले वस्त्र वान्धिया करे परनाम ॥ २२

जीओ जीओ रायत धर्म्म देउक वर ।
यत गुटि सागरेर वाला एत आरिव्वल ॥ २३
केने २ रायत सकल आइलेन कि कारन ॥ २४

केमन वुद्धि करि केमन चरिचर ।
असति राजा हइल राज्येर भितर ॥ २५
धेयाने वुड़ा सिव धेयान करे चाय् ।
छय् मासेर परमाइ राजार कपाले नागाल पाय् ॥ २६

---

१२ । कैल्ल = करिल ॥ १५ । छन = उच्छिन्न ॥ १७ । परामस = परामर्श ॥
१९ । वोला = भोला ॥ २२ । परनाम = प्रणाम ॥ २३ । आरिव्वल = आयुर्वल ॥
२६ । धेयाने = ध्यान । परमाइ = परमायुः । नागाल is connected with the dhátu
लग् ॥

मोर कथा कान यदि मयनार वरावर।
कैलाष्ठ भूवन मोर कर्व्वे नयड भयड ॥ २७

एक सत्य दुइ सत्य तिन सत्य हरि।
तोमार कथा यदि कव्यों मह्वा पापे मरि ॥ २८
येत रायत जन परामस करिया।
खीकबेर छाठत नागिया यान चलिया ॥ २९
धुप सिन्दुर नेन पातिल भरिया।
हांस कैतर नेन खाञ्चा भरिया ॥ ३०
धञोला पांठा नेन रसी साइङ्ग करिया।
रविवार दिन निरा थाकिया पारनी गङ्गा यान चलिया ॥ ३१
धर्म्मरे थान गङ्गा किनारे वान्धिया।
धञोला पांटा देन वालु छेद करिया ॥ ३२
हांस कत गुला देन घाटे उकरगिया।
धूप सिन्दुर देन घाटे ज्वालाइया ॥ ३३
अफिन्ना विन्नार धोय आने उपारिया।
नांटि चिपिया साप देन छाड़िया।
ए साप निले अच्चल पातिया ॥ ३४

रविवार दिन लोके सांचो दिल।
सोमवार दिन राजार ए ज्वरि करिल ॥ ३५
मङ्गलवार दिन राजा काह्निला पड़िल।
वुधवारे राजा अन्न पानि छाड़िल ॥ ३६
विसुदवारे राजा ए गुरु छाड़िल।
फिर मङ्गलवारे चित्र गोविन्द दफ्तर खुलिल ॥ ३७
मानिक चन्द्र राजार छय् मास परमाइ दफ्तर नागाइल पाइल।
वेन्ना मुख हैये समन राजाक वलिव र लागिल ॥ ३८

असति राजा हइल राज्येर भितर।
सेइ राजाक लैया आइस यमालयेर भितर ॥ ३९

२९। नागिया = लागिया ॥ ३१। निरा = निरम्न(?)। ३२। थान = स्थान ॥
३४। साप = शाप ॥ ३५। सांचो = शाप ॥

আবাল যমকে ডাকিবার লাগিল।
গোদা যমের নামে চিঠি হাওলাত করে দিল ॥ ৪০

তোক বলোঁ গোদা যম বাক্য মোর ধর।
হাতে গলে মানিক চন্দ্র রাজাক বান্ধিয়া হাজির কর ॥ ৪১
চামের দড়ি লোহার ডাঙ্গ নৈলে গিরো দিয়া।
তখনে গোদা যম চলিল হাঁটিয়া ॥ ৪২
কত দুরে যেয়ে গোদা কত পাক্কা পায়।
কতক যাইতে মানিক চন্দ্র রাজার বাড়ী পায় ॥ ৪৩
ছয় মাসের কাহিলা রাজা মহলের ভিতর।
তথোত খবর নাহি করে ময়না সুন্দর ॥ ৪৪

তোক বলোঁ যে নেঙ্গা যাত্র বাক্য মোর ধর।
এই কথা জানাও গিয়ে ময়নার বরাবর ॥ ৪৫
ছয় মাসের কাহিলা রাজা মহলের ভিতর।
দেখা করিবার চায় রাজ রাজেশ্বর ॥ ৪৬
এ কথা শুনিয়া নেঙ্গা না থাকিল রৈয়া।
ময়নার মহলে চলিল হাঁটিয়া ॥ ৪৭
আগ দুয়ারে ময়না মতি পসার খেলায়।
খিরকির দুয়ারে দিয়া পরনাম জানায় ॥ ৪৮

কেনে কেনে নেঙ্গা আইলেন কি কারন ॥ ৪৯

নেঙ্গা বলে সোন মা সোন সমাচার।
ছয় মাসের কাহিলা রাজা মহলের ভিতর ॥
দেখা করিবার চায় রাজ রাজেশ্বর ॥ ৫০
ধেয়ানে ময়না মতি ধেয়ান করে চায়।
ধেয়ানের মধ্যে যমের নাগাল পায় ॥ ৫১
আনিল বাঙ্গলা গুয়া মিঠাভরি পান।
এ বাঙ্গলা গুয়া কাটাইর দিয়া করে দুই খান ॥ ৫২
পানের বুকে চুনের নেওয়া দিয়া।
হেট খিলি উপর খিলি মাইল্লে তুলিয়া ॥ ৫৩

৪০। হাওলাত = حوالت ॥ ৪৪। তথোত = তাবৎ ॥ ৪৭। রৈয়া = রহিয়া ॥

घोल पुटि ह्यान दिले खिलित भरिया ।
पानेर वाटा वान्दिर माथाय दिया ॥ ५४
निकलिल मयना मति यात्रा करिया ।
ऐ राजार मह्वाले उत्तरिल गिया ॥ ५५

केने केने महाराजा डाकिले कि कारन ॥ ५६

छय मासेर काछिला राजा महलेर भितर ।
तत्त खवर ना करेन मयना सुन्दर ॥ ५७
मयना वले सोन राजा राज राजेश्वर ।
आमार सरीरेर ह्यान नेओ वोल सिकिया ।
आमार वसेर नदी कान्दे यावे सुखाइया ॥ ५८
आमार वयसे वड़ वृक्ष यावे मरिया ।
दुइ जने राजा कि करिम घर जुयान हइया ॥ ५९

राजा वले सुन मयना वाक्य मोर धर ।
एखनि मोर मानिक चन्द्र यमे लइया याउक ।
ताहातेओ स्त्रीर ह्यान गरवे ना सुनाउक ॥ ६०

नारीर ह्यान देखिया ह्याने करिल हेला ।
ठिक दुपर भाङ्‌या यम करिया गेल मेला ॥ ६१
मरन ठसा मारिल तुलिया ।
जल जल वलिया राजा उठिल कान्दिया ॥ ६२
जल खोओओ खोओओ मयना सुन्दर ।
एक झाड़ि जल दिया प्रान रक्षा कर ॥ ६३

एक सत रानी आछे महलेर भितर ।
तार ह्याते जल खाओ राज राजेस्वर ॥ ६४

एक सत रानीर हस्तेर जल आंइस टानि गोन्दाय ।
तोमार ह्याते जल खाइले वड भाग्य हय ॥ ६५

---

५८ । वसेर = वयसेर । कान्दे = स्कन्ध ॥ ६० । गरवे = गर्भ ॥ ६१ । दुपर = दुर प्रहर ॥

एलाय़ यदि आमि याइ जलक नागिय़ा ।
ऐत भाड़ुय़ा यम तोक लइय़ा यावे वान्धिय़ा ॥ ৬৬

राजा वले सुन मय़ना वाक्य मोर धर ।
तैल पाठेर खाड़ा थोओ विछानात फेलाय़ा ॥ ৬৭
यखन आसिवे भाड़ुय़ा यम दैत्त दानव हय़ा ॥
तैल पाठेर खाड़ा दिय़ा फेलामु काटिय़ा ॥ ৬৮
येन मते मय़ना मति हस्ते झाड़ि लैल ।
हांचि जिठि वाधा विस्तर पड़िल ॥ ৬৯
येन घड़ि मय़ना मति चतुरार वाहिर हइल ।
सात दिय़ा सात जना गर्ज्जिय़ा सेन्दाइल ॥ ৭০
चामेर दड़ा दिय़ा वान्धिल ।
लोहार मुद्गर दिय़ा डाङ्गाइवार लागिल ॥ ৭১

के मारेन आमाक विस्तर करिय़ा ।
मय़ना मति गेछे जलक नागिय़ा ।
एक झाड़ि जल खांओ उद्दर भरिय़ा ॥ ৭২

तोर माइय़ा पाइय़ाछे गोरक्षनाथेर वर ।
नागाइल पाइले मय़ना ना करे कुसल ॥
हाटुय़ा पाड़ि किलाइवे आमाक वेलार दुपर ॥ ৭৩
यमेर माइर सवार ना पारिय़ा ।
मय़ना वलिय़ा राजा दिल जीउ छाड़िय़ा ॥ ৭৪
ए जीउ निले गोदा यम नांठित वान्दिय़ा ।
सात दिय़ा सात जन गेल चलिय़ा ॥ ৭৫

एत मय़ना गङ्गार तीरे गेल चलिय़ा ॥
मय़ना वले सुन गङ्गा वलि निवेदन ॥ ৭৬
ये राजार पुजा खाइला ए वार वत्सर ।
एक झाड़ि जल दिय़ा प्रान रक्षा कर ॥ ৭৭
एक झाड़ि वदलि विय़ाल्लीस झाड़ि लओ ।
ताहाते धर्म्मि राजा जीउ वदला ओ ॥ ৭৮

৬৮। दैत्त = दैत्य ॥ ৭২। उद्दर = उदर ॥

कार वादे जल निया याञो झाड़ि भरिया।
सेत धर्म्मि राजाक् गेल धरिया॥ ७९
एइ कथा सुनिया मयना रोदन करिवार नागिल।
लच्छ टाकार झाड़ि पाकाइया फेलिल॥ ८०
चौद् ताल जलेर मध्ये मयना आसन करिल।
कपाले सिन्दुर मइलान देखिल॥ ८१
हातेर सांखा काल देखिल।
लच्छ टाकार दुइ मुठ सांखा मस्तके भाङ्गिल॥ ८२

स्वामि हारा हया रे। आर कत दिन रव चायारे॥ धुया॥ ८३

मह्लत लागिया मयना चलिल हाटिया।
येन मयना मति मन्दीरे सेन्दाइल॥
आग प्रदीप पाछ प्रदीप लागाइया दिल॥ ८४
यमालय् लागिया मयना चलिल हाटिया।
नदीर पारे मयना मति गेल चलिया॥ ८५
नदी देखिया मयना भयङ्कर हइल।
छय् मास ओसार नदी वछरत पड़े खेओया।
एक एक ढेउ उठे पर्व्वतेर चूड़ा॥ ८६

विधि आमार दुःखेर कपाल। येमन विन्दार गोपाल॥
भाङ्गा नौका छिड़ा काछि गुरु केमने हवे पाड़॥
यदि आमार गुरु सहाय् थाके॥ ८७
धरम हाइल धरे, भाङ्गा नौका छिड़ा काछि
गुरु लाइगाव किराने॥ धुया। ८८

परिधानेर साड़ी अर्द्ध खान मयना मती दिल जलत विछाया।
योग आसन धरिल मयना धरम सरन करिया॥ ८९
तुड़ु तुड़ु करिया मयना ऊङ्कार छाड़िल।
छय् मासेर दरिया छय् दण्डे पार हइल॥ ९०
यमपुरि लागिया चलिल हांटिया।
छत्रिस कुटि यम दरवार वसिछे॥ ९१

८३। स्वामि = स्वामी॥ ८६। वछरत = वत्सरे॥ ८८। किराने = کناری॥
८९। सरन = स्मरण॥ ९०। दरिया = دریا॥

येन मते मयना यमालय खाड़ा हइल ।
भिता भिति यम पालावार लागिल ॥ ९२
यमपुरि याया मयना पातिल धुम ।
कारो उठिल पेटेर विस कारो माथार घुम ॥ ९३
ओझा गुनिक हया विस झाड़िया नामाय ।
औसध करिवार आले जन जन पालाय ॥ ९४
येन मते गोदा यम मयनाके देखिल ।
आपनकार महलक लागिया ए दौड़ करिल ॥ ९५
आपनकार महले याया घरे नुकाइल ।
ऐटे हइते मयना मति दिसा हारा हइल ॥ ९६
धेयाने मयना मति धेयान करे चाय ।
धेयानेर मध्ये घरत लागाल पाय ॥ ९७
ओ रूप थुइल मयना एकतर करिया ।
माइलानी रूप हइल मुरत वदलाइया ।
गोदार महले चलिल हांटिया ॥ ९८
गोदा गोदा वैले मयना तुलिया छाड़े राओ । ९९
येन मते गोदा यम मयनाक देखिल ।
टाटि भाङ्गिया गोदा यम ए दौड़ करिल ॥ १००
मार मार वलिया मयना नि याय पिछिया ।
एक सत हालुया हाल वय निधुया पाथारे ॥
हरिन वलिया यमक नि याय पिछिया ॥ १०१
ऐठे हइते गोदा यम दिसा हारा हइल ।
इचला माछ हइये दरियाय झाप दिल ॥ १०२
धेयाने मयना मति धेयान करे चाय ।
धेयानेर मध्ये इचलार लागाल पाय ॥ १०३
तुड़ तुड़ करिया मयना ऊङ्कार छाड़िल ।
वेयाल्लिस भइस हइल मुरत वदलाइया ।
ए दरिया भइस पड़िल झम्प दिया ॥ १०४
खार खाइते२ यमक नि याय पिछिया ।
मध्य दरियात यमक धरिल ठासिया ॥ १०५

---

८४ । ओझा = उपाध्यायस्य ॥ ९६ । नुकाइल = लुकायित हइल ॥ ९८ । एकतर = एकत्र । मुरत = मूर्ति ॥ ९९ । राओ = रव ॥ १०१ । नि = लइया ॥

ऐत गोदा यम ख्याटिया़ वज्जर ।
डाइन पिड़ेर दख्ख भाङ्गिया़ उठिया़ दिल लड़ ॥ १०६
ऐटे हइते गोदा यम दिसा हारा हइल ।
छेफलां मत्स हइया़ जलत भासिवार लागिल ॥ १०७
ओ रूप थुइल मयना एकतर करिया़ ।
पानकाउड़ि वानोया़र हइल मुरत वदलाइया़ ॥ १०८
पाखार साटते नि याय़ पिट्टिया़
मध्य दरिया़ गोदा यमक धरिल ठोकाइया़ ॥ १०९
ऐत गोदा यम ख्याटिया़ वज्जर ।
ढेकेया़ फेलाइया़ मयनाक् दिल लहड़ ॥ ११०
ऐटे हइते गोदा यम कोन काम करिल ।
गचि मच्छ हया़ कादात मिसाइल ॥ १११
ऐटे हइते मयना मति ध्येया़न करे चाय़ ।
ध्येया़नेर मध्ये कादात लागाल पाय़ ॥ ११२
तुड़ु तुड़ु करिया़ मयना ऊङ्कार छाड़िल ।
राजहांस हइया़ काद जारितेर गोदा यमक नि याय़ पिट्टिया़ ।
मध्य दरिया़त गोदा यमक धरिल ठासिया़ ॥ ११३
ढेकेया़ फेलाया़ मयना मतिक पालाइल छाड़िया़ ।
ओ रूप थुइल गोदा यम एकतर करिया़ ॥ ११४
घुगड़िर रूप हइल मुरत वदलाइया़ ।
पातालक लागिया़ गेल चलिया़ ॥ ११५
पातालक याया़ मोचड़ाय़ यम दाड़ि ।
एखन कि चिनिवे मोक मयना मति साली ॥ ११६
ध्येया़ने मयना मति ध्येया़न करे चाय़ ।
ध्येया़नेर मध्ये मयना घुगड़िर लागाल पाय़ ॥ ११७
ओ रूप थुइल मयनः एकतर करिया़ ।
तेलङ्गा रूप हइल मयना मुरत वदलाइया़ ॥ ११८
पाताल भुवनत नागिया़ गेल चलिया़ ।
ऐटे याया़ गोदा यमक धरिल ठांसिया़ ।
छोनेक छोनेक करिया़ यमक उठाइल टानिया़ ॥ ११९

---

१०६ । वज्जर = वज्र ॥

ओ रूप थुइल मयना एकतर करिया।
आपनार रूप हइल मुरत वदलाइया॥ १२०
उपर कैरे फेलेया यमक किलिवार लागिल।
किलाइते किलाइते हात हापसाइल॥
चितर करिया फेलाइया यमक नेदावार लागिल॥ १२१
एत गोदा यम आंटिया वज्जर।
घड़ानी कैतर हइये सर्गे उड़े गेल॥ १२२
सिकिरा वाज हइल मयना मुरत वदलाइया।
आकास हइते गोदा यमक फेलाइल टालिया॥ १२३
एटा हइते गोदा यम दिस हारा हइया।
सलेयार रूप हइल मुरत वदलाइया॥ १२४
कठिया तेलीर वाड़ीक नागिया गेल चलिया।
कठिया तेलीर माचात थाकिल वसिया॥ १२५
धेयाने मयना मती धेयान कैरे चाय।
धेयानेर मध्ये सलेयार नागाल पाय॥ १२६
ओ रूप थुइल मयना एकतर करिया।
विलाइ रूप हइल मयना मुरत वदलाइया॥ १२७
एक विलाइर वदली वियाल्लिस विलाइ हइया।
कठिया तेलीर घर लइल घेड़िया॥ १२८
एक दण्ड दुइ दण्ड तिन दण्ड हइल।
सुवोधिया गोदा यमक कुवोधिया नागाल पाइल॥ १२९
माचा हइते गोदा यमक म्रत्तिकाय नामाइल।
टरकिया याया मयना मती गरदानात धरिल॥ १३०
एत गोदा यम आंटिया वज्जर।
आङ्गलेर सान्दि दिया उठिया दिल लहड़॥ १३१
ओ रूप थुइल यम एकतर करिया।
वैष्णव रूप हइल यम मुरत वदलाइया॥ १३२
काकड़ार माटिया लइल चन्दन करिया।
साइलेर फल लइल माला करिया॥ १३३
एरण्डार ठाल लइल आसा करिया।
सेवार वाड़ीक नागिया गेल चलिया।

१२२। सर्गे = स्वर्गे ॥ १३० । गरदानात = گردن میں ॥ १३४ । एण्डार = एरण्डेर ॥

यत वैष्णवेर मध्यत रहइल वसिया ॥ १३४
धेयाने मयना मती धेयान करे चाय ।
धेयानेर मध्ये वैष्णवेर लागान पाय ॥ १३५
ओ रूप थुइल मयना एकतर करिया ।
मौ माछि हइल मयना मुरत वदलाइया ॥ १३६
एक माछिर वदली वियाल्लिस माछि हया ।
सेवार वाड़ीक मागिया गेल चलिया ।
यत वैष्णवेर माथार उपर वेड़ाय घुरिया ॥ १३७
वैष्णव सकल वले भाइ सोन समाचार ।
कोन वैष्णव अपराधी आछेन सभार माझ ॥ १३८
येन मते गोदा यम माछि देखिल ।
वैष्णवेर कँथार तलत् सन्दाइल ॥ १३९
येन मते मयना मति सन्दाम देखिल ।
उड़ाओ दिया यमेर घाड़त पड़िल ॥ १४०
माछिर कामड़ सइवार ना पारिया ।
गोदा यम पालाइल छाड़िया ॥ १४१
माछि रूप थुइल मयना एकतर करिया ।
आपनार रूप हइल मुरत वदलाइया ॥ १४२
येत गोदा यमक धरिल पिट्टिया ।
एक पांजा एलुया खेड़ आनिल उकाड़िया ॥ १४३
वान पुटि कुचनि पाकाय तेपथीत वसिया ।
मयनार कमड़े यमेर कमड़े वान्दने वान्दिया ।
हातेर हेमतालेर लाठि दिया नि याय डाङ्गाइया ॥ १४४
मयना वले सुन यम वलि निवेदन ।
आमार स्वामी धन देओ आर छाड़िया ॥ १४५
तोमार स्वामी धन आमि ना दिव छाड़िया ।
एटे हइते मयना मति रोदन करते लागिल ॥ १४६
आमार पति नाइ घरे रे दीननाथ
आमि कार लछे रवरे नविन वसते ॥ धुया ॥ १४७

---

१३६ । मौ माछि = मधु मक्षिका ॥ १३८ । माझ = मध्ये ॥ १४१ । सइवार = सहिवार ॥ १४४ । वाम = वाओयाम = हापंचापत् । तेपथीत = विपथे ॥

তুড়ু তুড়ু করিয়া ময়না ঊঙ্কার ছাড়িল ।
যত মনি গনক ঊঙ্কারে নামাইল ॥ ১৪৮
পুষ্প রথে গোরক বিদ্যাধর ।
ঢেকি বাহনে নামিল নারদ মুনিবর ॥ ১৪৯
বাসায়ার পিটিত নামিল ভোলা মহেশ্বর ।
ধনুক বানে নামি গেল শ্রীরাম লক্ষন ॥ ১৫০
পাঁচ ভাই পাণ্ডব নামিল ঠাঁই ঠাঁই ।
যত সত মুনি নামিল তার লেখা যোখা নাই ॥ ১৫১
মাথার চুল ময়না দুই আধ করিয়া ।
গোরক নাথের চরনত পড়িল ভজিয়া ॥ ১৫২

রক্ষা কর রক্ষা কর গোরক বিদ্যাধর ।
আমার স্বামি ধন আনিছে ধরিয়া ॥

আমার স্বামি ধনক না দেয় ছাড়িয়া । ২৫৩
গোরক নাথ বলে সোন সোমাচার ॥
যত মুনি গন পরামর্স করিয়া ।
ময়নাক আসীর্ব্বাদ দেয় ॥ ১৫৪
যা যা ময়না তোমাক দিলাম বর ।
সাত মাসি ছেলে হৌক উদরের ভিতর ॥ ১৫৫
যেন মতে মুনিগন আসীর্ব্বাদ দিল ।
সোলার মত আছিল সরীর ক্রমে ভারি হইয়া গেল ॥ ১৫৬

আঠার মাসে জন্ম উনিস বৎসরে মরন ।
সিতাব করি ভজে ছাড়ির চরন ।
এ গুরু ভজিলে না হবে মরন ॥ ১৫৭
এ কথা সুনিয়া ময়না না থাকিল রয়া ।
আপনকার মহলত নাইগে উতরিল গিয়া ॥ ১৫৮
নআো কড়া কড়ি নিল হস্তত করিয়া ।
গঙ্গার কুলে গেল চলিয়া ॥ ১৫৯
নআো কড়া কড়ি দিয়া মৃত্তিকা কিনি নিল ।
আপন মহলক লাগিয়া গমন করিল ॥ ১৬০

---

১৪৮ । মনি = মুনি ॥ ১৫০ । বাসায়ার = ? বৃষভ ॥ ১৫৭ । সিতাব = ? شتاب

वुड़ा घर भाङ्गिया वेगारि साजाइल ।
साइङ्गे साइङ्गे खड़ी याइते लागिल ॥ १६१
तैल घृत सरिसा तिल यावार लागिल ।
यत ज्ञाति सग आनिल राओ दिया ॥
कांचा वांस काटिया मञ्चलि साजाइल ॥ १६२
धर्म्मि राजाक निल मञ्चलि साजाइया ।
मयना मति चड़े कओयाइरक लागाइया ॥ १६३
हरिगुन गान मयना गाइवार लागिल ।
सङ्कीर्त्तन करिवार लागिल नदीर पाच्छार लागि गमन करिल ॥ १६४
उत्तर दक्षिने चिता आरोपिल ।
खुटि गाड़िया माचान पातिल ॥ १६५
खुटिर वगले २ वसाइया गेल घृतेर हाड़ि ।
तार निचे वसाइया गेल तैलेर झाड़ी ।
सरिसा तिल गुला दिल छिटाइया ॥ १६६
गुरु गुरु वलिया मयना ऊङ्कार छाड़िल ।
साक्षात गोरक नाथ आसिया खाड़ा हइल ॥ १६७

रक्षा कर रक्षा कर गोरक विद्याधर ।

याओ याओ मयना तोमाक दिनु वर ॥
माघ मासिया जार लागिवे अनलेर भितर ॥ १६८
कपाल भर्त्ति सिन्दुर मयना परिते लागिल । १६९
पाटेर साड़ी मयना परिधान करिया ।
सुवर्न काटारि आमेर ठाल निल हस्तेते करिया ।
उत्तर दक्षिने राजाक निल सोताइया ॥ १७०
मयनार डाइन हस्तेते राजा सितान दिल ।
राजार वाम हस्त मयना सितान दिल ॥ १७१
एकखान करिया खड़ी दिल नगरि घरे घरे ।
आकास जमिने खड़ी ठेक लागिल ॥ १७२
चोया चन्दन छिटाइल चन्द्र सदागर ।
अनल लागाइया दिते नाइ एक रति ॥ १७३

दुयारेर आगत छिल गुरु पारनेर घर ।

তাঁয় উকা তুলে দিল হস্তর উপর ॥ ১৭৪
যত জ্ঞাস্তা সকল এক ছাড়ী জল দিয়া ।
সাইক্ষত করিয়া এক যাক দুই যাক পাঁচ যাক দিল ।
হরি বোল বলিয়া আনল লাগাইয়া দিল ॥ ১৭৫
যত ঘড়ী ব্রহ্মা ছতের বাস যাইল ।
ধাঁ ধাঁ করিয়া অনল জ্বলিবার লাগিল ॥ ১৭৬
সাত দিন নঅো রাইত ময়না অনলের ভিতর ।
পুড়িতে পোড়া না যায় পরিধানের কাপড় ॥ ১৭৭
ধর্ম্মি রাজাক পোড়াইয়া ময়না কোলাতে কৈল ছাই ।
এেত ময়না বৈসে আছে যেন ঘরের গোসাই ॥ ১৭৮
ধর্ম্মি রাজাক পোড়াইয়া সর্গে উঠিল ধুয়া ।
বৈসে আছে ময়না মতি যেন কাঁচা সোনা ॥ ১৭৯
ছোট জ্ঞাস্তা উঠে বলে বড় জ্ঞাস্তা ভাই ।
ফিক দেঅো ফিক দেঅো জ্ঞাস্তা সকল ॥ ১৮০
ময়না মতী বৈসে আছে অনলের ভিতর ।
ময়না বলে সুন জ্ঞাস্তা সাত মাসী ছেলে আছে উদরের ভিতর ॥
ফিক না দেন জ্ঞাস্তা সকল ॥ ১৮১
ছোট জ্ঞাস্তা উঠে বলে বড় জ্ঞাস্তা ভাই ।
চান্দের বরাবর চল চলিয়া যাই ॥ ১৮২
ছোট হইতে জান তোরা চান্দ সদাগর ।
কি জোয়াব দেয় আমার বরাবর ॥ ১৮৩
আগ দুয়ারে সদাগর পসার খেলায় ।
খেরকির দুয়ার দিয়া প্রনাম যোগায় ॥ ১৮৪

কেনে কেনে জ্ঞাস্তা সকল আইলা কি কারন ॥ ১৮৫

সাত দিন নঅো রাইত ময়না অনলের ভিতর ।
তবু পোড়া নাই যায় ময়না সুন্দর ॥ ১৮৬

এে ময়না পাইয়াছে গোরক নাথের বর ।
আনলত পোড়া না যায় জলত না হয় তল ॥
তিন ভুবন টলিয়া গেল না যায় যমের ঘর ।

---

১৭৪ । উকা = উল্কা ॥   ১৭৮ । বৈসে আছে = বসিয়াছে ॥

ताक मारिवार चाओ छाल्ता सकल ॥ १८७
वाओयान्न कुटि कोचड़ा पाकाओ तेयथित वसिया ।
वाइस मोन पसान नेओ साइङ्ग करिया ॥ १८८
ऊलिया गुतिया नेओ वाह्लेर करिया ।
वाइस मोन पासान देओ वुकत वान्धिया ॥ १८९
आङ्गरार समते मयनाक देओ वोल भासाइया ।
छिनान करिया याओ मह्लत लागिया ॥ १९०
ए कथा सुनिया छाल्ता ना थाकिल रैया ।
वाइस मोन पासान लैल साइङ्ग करिया ॥ १९१
मयना मतिक वाह्रिर करिल ऊलिया गुतिया ।
वाइस मोन पासान दिल वुकत वान्धिया ॥ १९२
आङ्गरार सा मल मयनाक दिल भासाइया ।
छिनान करिया छाल्ता गेल चलिया ॥ १९३

आठार मास आठार दिन मयनार गेल पुरिया ।
एत धर्म्मि राजा करट फिरिल ।
मैह्लाम मैह्लाम वलिया मयना कान्दिवार लागिल ॥ १९४
खरपा छान मयना मारिल तुलिया ।
वाओयान्न कुटि कोचड़ा फेलाइल काटिया ॥ १९५
मैह्लाम मैह्लाम वलिया मयना निम तरु तले उठिल ।
छाड़िया कोने येन देओया गर्ज्जिल ॥ १९६
फुले जले महाराज म्त्तिकाय पड़िल ।
चोंया चोंया करिया तिनि राओ काड़िल ॥ १९७
छोट छाल्ता उठे वले वड़ छाल्ता भाइ ।
किसेर छेले कान्दे चल देखिवार याइ ॥ १९८
एक पाय दुइ पाय आइल चलिया ।
मयना वले सुन छाल्ता मोर वुद्धि धर ॥ १९९
वड़ राजार पालकी आन साजाइया ।
छाओयाल राजाक नेओ मह्लक लागिया ॥ २००
वड़ ये पालकी आनाइल साजाइया ।
धर्म्मि राजाक नइल पालकीत चड़ाइया ॥ २०१

---

१९४ । मैह्लाम = मरिलाम ॥

ঢাক ঢোল তমবুরা কাঁসি বাজে ঠাঁই ঠাঁই।
কারতাল ভেঁউড় মুর্চ্ছল বাজে ঠাঁই ঠাঁই॥ ২০২
বন্দুকের ধুরা ধুরি ধুমায় অন্ধকার।
বাপে পুতক না চিনে ডাকা ডাকি সার॥ ২০৩
কাঙ্গালের কেলে হইল রাজ্যের ভিতর।
অন্ন জল দিবার না পারে মহলের ভিতর॥ ২০৪
ফুলে জলে ফেলিয়া আইল তে পথির উপর। ২০৫
উ ঝো ক্লেক নৈল ময়না কোলাত করিয়া।
মহলক লাগিয়া গেল চলিয়া॥ ২০৬

তোক বলো বান্দো বাক্য মোর ধর। ২০৭
দাইয়ানির মহলক লাগিয়া গেল চলিয়া।
দাইয়ানিক আনিল ডাক দিয়া॥ ২০৮
দোনো ক্লোর নাড়ি ক্লেদ করিল বসিয়া।
যত কিছু দান দিল দাইয়ানিক লাগিয়া।
দাইয়ানি গেল মহলক লাগিয়া॥ ২০৯
আজি আজি কালি কালি করিয়া সাত দিন হইল।
সাত দিন পর্য্যন্ত রাজা সাদিনা কোরাইল॥ ২১০
আজি আজি কালি কালি করিয়া দস দিন হইল।
দস দিন পরে রাজা এ দসা করিল॥ ২১১
ত্রিস দিনে রাজা ত্রিসা করিল, সংকীর্ত্তন করিবার লাগিল।
জ্ঞাতা সকল আসিয়া যজ্ঞ করিল॥ ২১২
যত জ্ঞাতি সকলক ভোজন করাইল।
তদ ঘড়ি ময়না মতি মত্স পরস করিল॥ ২১৩
আজি আজি কালি কালি করিয়া এক বত্সর হইল।
এক বত্সর বাদে এক দিন আসিল॥ ২১৪
আজি কালি করিয়া পাঁচ বত্সর হইল।
গুরুর নিকটে পড়িবার দিল॥ ২১৫
চারি কলমে রাজাক লিখা সিখাইল।
আজি কালী করিয়া সাত বত্সর হইল॥ ২১৬
নাম রাজার তখনই রাখিল।

২০৯। নাড়ি = নাভি॥ ২১৩। মত্স = মত্স্য। পরস = স্পর্শ॥

মানিক চন্দ্র রাজার বেটা গোপি চন্দ্র হইল ॥ ২১৭
তাহার ছোট ভাইয়ের নাম খেতুয়া লঙ্কেশ্বর ॥ ২১৮
আজি কালী করিয়া নভো বৎসর হইল।
তখনি ময়না মতি কোন কাম করিল ॥ ২১৯
গুরু ব্রাহ্মনের সাইক্ষাত কথা বলিবার লাগিল ॥ ২২০

যা যা গুরু ব্রাহ্মন বাক্য আমার লও।
হরি চন্দ্র রাজার কাছে সীঘ্র করিয়া যাও ॥ ২২১
তার ঘরে আছে অদুনা পদুনা কন্যা দুইজন।
তার আছে কন্যা দুই জন মহলের ভিতর।
এ কন্যা যুড়িয়া আইস বলিলাম তোমায় ॥ ২২২
এ কথা সুনিয়া ব্রাহ্মন ঠাকুর না থাকিল রৈয়া।
হরি চন্দ্র রাজার বাড়ী গেল চলিয়া ॥ ২২৩
হরি চন্দ্র রাজা বলিয়া তুলিয়া ছাড়ে রাও।
ঘরে ছিল হরি চন্দ্র রাজা বাহিরে দিলে পাও ॥ ২২৪
পণ্ডিত ঠাকুর বলিয়া করে প্রনাম ॥ ২২৫
দিব্য সিংহাসন বসিবার দিল।
কর্পুর তাম্বুল দিয়া জিজ্ঞাসা করিল ॥ ২২৬
কেনে কেনে গুরু ব্রাহ্মন এত দুর গমন ॥ ২২৭

ময়না পাঠাইয়া দিল তোমার বরাবর।
তোমার ঘরে কন্যা আছে অদুনা পদুনা।
তাক যুড়িবার চায় ময়না সুন্দর ॥ ২২৮
ময়নার পুত্র আছে মহলের ভিতর।
তাকে বিয়া দিবার চায় ময়না সুন্দর ॥ ২২৯

যা যা বলিয়া তাকে হুকুম দিল।
এ কথা সুনিয়া ব্রাহ্মন ময়নার মহলে গেল ॥ ২৩০
ভারে লইল গুয়া সাইঙ্গে লইল পান।
গুয়া পান কাটিবার গেল ব্রাহ্মন পঞ্চ জন ॥ ২৩১
গুয়া পান কাটিয়া সুভাসুভ বুঝিল।
বিবাহের দিন তখনই করিল ॥ ২৩২

২২০। সাইক্ষাত = সাক্ষাৎ ॥

सनिवार दिना मयना अधिवास दिल ।
रविवार दिना विवाह करिवार साजिल ॥ २३३
पञ्च गाछि कलार गाछ हरिचन्द्र राजार महलत गाड़िल ।
सोनाली चालुन वाति तखनइ धराइल ॥ २३४
पञ्च वैराती तखनइ आनिल डाक दिया ।
उलु उलु सब्द करिवार लागिल ॥ २३५
अदुनाक दिया विवाह दिल पदुनाक दिल दाने ।
एक सत वान्दी दिले व्यावहार कारने ॥ २३६
एक सत तालुक दिल दाने धरिया ।
एक सत हस्ति दिल दाने धरिया ॥ २३७
एक सत घोड़ा दिल दाने धरिया ।
एक सत गावि दिल दाने धरिया ॥ २३८
विवाह दिया राजाक विदाय दिल ।
तखनइ मयना मति यत राज्येर राजाक निमन्त्रन करिल ॥ २३९

सेइत धर्म्मि राजा गोपी चन्द्र पाट दिल । २४०

आठार वरिसे गोपि चन्द्र राजा ।
वृद्ध मातार आज्ञाय सन्यास हइये याय ॥ २४१
एक सत सुन्दरी कान्दे चरन धरिया ।
एत धर्म्मि राजा ना याओ छाड़िया ॥ २४२

ना याइओ ना याइओ राजा दुर देसान्तर ।
कारे लागिया वान्दिलाम सीतल मन्दीर घर ॥ २४३
वान्दिलाम वाङ्गला घर नाइ पाड़ काली ।
एमन वयसे छाड़ि याओ आमार वृथा गावुरानी ॥ २४४
निन्देर सपने राजा हव दरिसन ।
पालङ्के फेलाइव हस्त नाइ प्रानेर धन ॥ २४५
दस गिरिर माओ वइन रवे स्यामि लइवे कोले ।
आमि नारी रोदन करिव खाली घर मन्दीरे ॥ २४६
खाली घर जोड़ा टाटि मारे लाठिर घा ।
वयस काले युवती राड़ी निते कलङ्क राओ ॥ २४७

---

२४४ । गावुरानी अर्थात् गर्भिन्यवस्था ॥ २४६ । रवे = रहिवे ॥ २४७ । निते = नित्यं ॥

आमाक सङ्गे करि लइया याञो ॥ २४८

जीवर जीवन धन आमि कन्या सङ्गे गेले ।

रान्धिया दिमु अन्न चुधार काले ॥ २४९

पियासार काले दिमु पानी ।

हांसिया खेलिया पोहामु रजनी ॥ २५०

आइल पातार दखिले कथा कहिया यामु ।

गिरि लोकर वाड़ी गेले गुव स्याम वलिमु ॥ २५१

सितल पाटि विछाइया दिमु वालीसे हेलान पाञो ।

हाउस रङ्गे यातिमु हस्त पाञो ॥ २५२

हात खानि दुःख हइले पाञो खानि यातिमु ।

एरङ्गर कौतुकर वेला सुति भुञ्जिमु, एसुति भुञ्जाइमु ॥ २५३

ग्रीस काले वदनत दिमु दण्ड पाखार वाञो ।

माघ मासि सिते घेसिया रमु गाञो ॥ २५४

माघ मासि सिते सित मरिचर झोल ।

इन्द्र मिठा भूषाइमु एक सत नारीर कोल ॥ २५५

राजा वले सुन कन्या हरि चन्द्रर वेटि ।

कत रङ्गे कर माया सइवार ना पराि॥ २५६

वंस हरिर गुया खाइये दन्त करिले लोला ।

कथा कहिते ज्वले दन्त गुञ्जरे भमरा ॥ २५७

नारी हवु चाकन चिकन पुरुस कैञ्था ओड़ा ।

दस गिरस्त वलिवे अथीत नारी चोरा ॥ २५८

नारी चोरा अथीत वैले गिरस्त ना दिवे ठांइ ।

तोर आमार वङुयार वेटि कहिवार सञ्जात नाइ ॥ २५९

रानी वले सुन राजा विलातेर नागर ।

एक निवेदन करि तोमार वरावर ॥ २६०

तोमार नाकान राम खिलिका गलार माझत दिया ।

तोमार नाकान डोर कपिन वान्धिमु भिंड़िया ॥ २६१

दुइ तन वान्धिमु नेते धोरा दिया ।

छामुर छयटा दन्त फेलाइमु भाङ्गिया ।

२५४। ग्रीस = ग्रीष्म ॥ २५८। गिरस्त = गृहस्थ। अथीत = अतीत ॥ २६०। विलातेर = ولايت ॥ २६१। नाकान = ? न्याय ॥ २६२। तन = स्तन ॥

আউ টাক মাথার কেস মুই ফেলাম্মো মুড়িয়া ॥ ২৬২
হাতত তুম্বা গলাত কেন্থা উদাসীনী হমু ।
তোমার পাছে২ গিয়া ভিক্ষা মাগি খামু ॥ ২৬৩

স্যামের বাসিরে মন মজালুরে রয়া রয়া নয়ান ঝোরে ॥ ধুয়া ॥ ২৬৪

রাজা বলে জয় বিধি ঠেকিতু মযা জালে ।
কি আমার প্রেমটা হইলো স্ত্রীলোকর সঙ্গে ॥ ২৬৫
মোর সঙ্গে যাবু না অথীতর সঙ্গে যাবে ।
সেটে আছে বনর বাঘ দেখিয়া ডড়াবে ॥
সেটে আছে বনর বাঘ দুর্জন বাঘর ভয় ॥ ২৬৬
স্ত্রী আর পুরুসে যদি পথ বহয়া যায় ।
হেন দুঃখে বোনর বাঘে স্ত্রীক ধরিয়া খায় ॥ ২৬৭
খাবে আর না খাবে বাঘে ফেলাইবে মারিয়া ।
কেনে আর মরিবি তুই অথীতর লগে যায়া ॥ ২৬৮

খল খল করিয়া কন্যা হাসিবার লাগিল ।

কে কয় এ গুলা কথা কে আর পইতায় ॥ ২৬৯
পুরুসর সঙ্গে গেলে কি স্ত্রীক বাঘে ধরে খায় ।
ও গুলা কথা ভুট মুট পালাবার উপায় ॥ ২৭০
খায়না কেনে বোনর বাঘে তাক নাই ডর ।
নিত কলঙ্কে মরন হউক স্বামির পদতল ॥ ২৭১
তুমি হবু বট বৃক্ষ আমি তোমার লতা ।
রাজ্ঞা চরন বেড়িয়া লমু পালাইয়া যাবু কোথা ॥ ২৭২
যখন আছিনু আমি মা বাপর ঘরে ।
তখন কেনে ধর্ম্মি রাজা না গেলেন সন্ন্যাসি হইয়ে ॥ ২৭৩
এখন হইতু রূপর নারী তোরে যোগ্যমান ।
মোকে ছাড়িয়া হবু সন্ন্যাস মুই তেজিম পরান ॥ ২৭৪
তোমারে আগে কাল যৌবন মোর পড়ুক গড়িয়া ।
পাকিলে মাথার চুল যাবেন সন্ন্যাস হইয়া ॥ ২৭৫
এ রঙ্গ মালতীর ঘরে লইয়া পড়ে ডাল ।
নারী হইয়ে রঙ্গ রূপ রাখিমু কত কাল ॥ ২৭৬

---

২৭৪ । তেজিম = ত্যাগ করিব ॥

কত কাল রাখিমু যৌবন বান্দিয়া ছান্দিয়া।
নিরবধি ওড়ে প্রান স্বামী বলিয়া॥ ২৭৭

আমাক বিবাহ করিয়া যাও বল চলিয়া কান্দো তোমার লাগি।
তোমার আছে বাপ ভাই মোর অভাগিনীর কেউ নাই।
আমি ছেড়ে এলেম তোর রাজার কারনে॥ ধুয়া॥ ২৭৮

অদুনা পদুনা বান্ধিয়া বিবাহ করিল।
ভাট ব্রাহ্মন দিয়া অদুনা নাম থুইল॥ ২৭৯
অদুনা নাম থুইল দাসী দিল সঙ্গে।

এমন পিরিতি ঘর ভাঙ্গিমু কেমনে॥ ২৮০
কোন দরজায় ভিক্ষা লয়ে কোন দরজায় যামু।
বানিয়া জাতি ছোটি কুল হেলাতে হারামু॥ ২৮১
আমার নাবালক সুন্দর কন্যা যেখানত দেখিমু।
ঝুরিয়া ঝুরিয়া সেই স্থানত মরিমু॥ ২৮২
তোমার নাকান সুন্দর কন্যা যেখানত দেখিমু।
আগে মা দাও দিয়া পশ্চাত ভিক্ষা লমু॥ ২৮৩

হায় হায় স্বামি ধন কাড়িলু কাল রাও।
চেঙ্গড়া কালে বিবাহ করে যুবায় ছাড়িয়া যাও॥ ২৮৪
ইও কাল থাক হৃদে লৈয়া হাত।
যাবত্ ঘুরিয়া আসি বত্সর পঞ্চাস॥ ২৮৫
মাথা তুলিয়া দেখ রাজা ডাব নারিকল।
হৃদয় উপরত সোভা করে গুয়া নারিকল॥ ২৮৬
হাতে ছিড়িমু মুখত দিমু গায় নাই তোর বল।
আছিল ফল যে পুরুস না খায় চৌদ্দ গোষ্ঠা রসাতলে যায়॥ ২৮৭

রাজা বলে সুন কন্যা হরি চন্দ্রর বেটা।
কথা ভাঙ্গি কথা বলিলে ও কথার মান যায়॥ ২৮৮
আগে চড়ে হস্তির মাহুত পিছে চড়ে রাজা।
হাটিয়া দেখিনু বড় বাঙ্গলা পথে অনেক দুর॥ ২৮৯

১৮০। পিরিতি = প্রীতি॥

खेये बुझिनु नारिकलर फल पेट नाइ भरे ।
मिछे थाकि गिरिर वेटा भेरन खाटिया मरे ॥ २९०

रानी वले सुन राजा रसिक नागर ।
एक खानि निवेदन करि तोमार वरावर ॥ २९१
याइस ना धर्म्मि राजा परदेसक नागिया ।
एकटि छेले दिया याओ कोलाक नागिया ॥ २९२
नालिमु पालिमु छेले कोलात करिया ।
पुत्र धनक देखिया तोमाक पासरिमु ॥ २९३
तोमार माथार छत्र दण्ड पुत्रर माथामु दिया ।
नया राजार मा वलिया राज्य खाइम वसिया ॥ २९४
छेलेर कथा वलिले रानी छेलेर कथा सुनिया । २९५

चिनि चाम्पा कला नय जलत माखि खामु ।
गाछर फल नय छिड़िया हस्तत दिमु ॥ २९६
तोमार कपालत छेले नाइ आमि कि करिमु ॥ २९७
पूर्व्वकाली गुरुर ज्ञान हृदये जपिया ।
सात मासि छेले हइ काया वदलाइया ॥ २९८
कोलात वसाइया कन्या आमाक वलिस पुत ।
फेलाओ रानी हृदयर वसन राजा खाउक दुद ॥ २९९

आमि वलिनु छेलेर कथा तुमि चाइलेन दुद ।
विवाहिता स्वामि हओ केमने वलि पुत ॥ ३००
तोमार गरवत छिल राजा भेड़ा छगाल ।
काड़ि काड़ार वुद्धि नाइ सरीरर भितर ॥ ३०१
आप्त राड़ी देखिया वधुक राड़ी करे ।
वाड़ीर आगे भातारटि गेले चक्षु पाकेया मरे ॥ ३०२

हां हां वड़यार वेटि माक दिल गाली ।
रनु हय दिन चारिक सन्न्यास हमु काली ॥ ३०३
कन्यार पेंटा सइवार ना पारिया ।
दरवार लागिया गेल राजा दुलालिया ॥ ३०४

---

२९० । मिछे = मिथ्ये अर्थात् वृथा ॥ २९३ । पासरिमु = ? स्मर्ण करिव ॥
२९८ । काया = काय ॥ २९९ । दुद = दुग्ध ॥

वार गछि गुया़ तेर गछि ताल ।
तार तले वसिल राजार छाओयाल ॥ ২০৫
ब्राह्मन सज्जन वसिल सारि सारि ।
मुल्लुकार हिसाव देय् विर सिं भाण्डारि ॥ ২০৬
सोनार खाटे थाकि मयना रुपार खाटे पाओ ।
सुपुत्रर दरवारत गेल मयना मति माओ ॥ ২০৭
भर काचारि करे डाम्बा डौल ।
हेन पति खाड़ा हइल मयना सुन्दर ॥ ২০৮
जननीक देखिया़ राजा करे परनाम ।
गलात वस्त्र वान्धिया़ करे परनाम ॥ ২০৯

जीओ जीओ राड़ी वेटा धर्म्मे देउक वर ।
यत गुटि सागरर वाला एत आरिव्वल ॥ ২১০
सुइ वुझ राड़ीर वेटा गेछें सन्न्यास हयया़ ।
आइज पति आछे सुन्दर वधु पायया़ ॥ ২১১
सत्य गेल दोया़ यइल तिरतिया़ हइले ।
कलि युग पड़े वेटा विवाह सकाले ॥ ২১২
कलि काल मन्द काल यइल आसिया़ ।
परार धन परे खाय् एकेला वसिया़ ॥ ২১৩
राजा हइये ना करे राज्यर विचार ।
पुत्र हइये ना करे पितार उद्धार ॥ ২১৪
स्त्री हइये ना करे स्वामीर भक्ति ।
सीष्ठ हइये ना करे गुरुर आरति ॥ ২১৫
चारिटा भाण्ड तार गेल अधगति ॥ ২১৬
गुरु ना भजिले भाण्ड श्मशाने ना खाय् ।
अराविष्णु देहा हइले कागा छाड़ि याय् ॥ ২১৭
आगुने पड़िले भाण्ड हय् छाड़ खार ।
जलत भासेया़ दिले मत्सर आहार ॥ ২১৮
मृत्तिकाय् गाड़िले भाण्ड पोकार आहार ।
कोन दिया़ ना देखों तोर भाण्डर निस्तार ॥ ২১৯

---

২০৬ । मुल्लुकार = ملکا ॥ ২০৭ । दरवारत = دربارمین ॥ ২০৮ । ২১১ । पति = प्रति ॥ ২১২ । दोया़ = द्वितीय ॥ ২১৭ । कागा = काक । cf. the Braj Bháshá काग ॥

वाक्षा निल कमलेरे केमन करे।
अथीतेर सङ्ग याञो। लोके वलिवे।
इनि छेलेर वुभि माञो नाइरे॥ धुया॥ ३२०

सन्न्यास करिते राजा करे गेल मन।
चौपथर माभत कन्या जुड़िल कान्दन॥ ३२१
केमन करे येते चाञो परदेस लागिया।
केमन ज्ञान आछे मयनार नेञो परखिया॥ ३२२
तैल परिच्छा देञो मयनार वरावर॥
ऐ परिच्छाय याय यदि उत्तरिया।
मस्तक मुड़िया तवे याञो सन्न्यास हइया॥ ३२३
एइ कथा सुनिया राजा ना थाकिल रैया।
दरवार लागिया राजा गेल चलिया॥ ३२४
दरवारे वसिया राजा वेचरित मन।
दयार भाइ गोलाम खेतुक डाके घने घन॥ ३२५

तोरे वलों गोलाम खेतुक वाक्य मोर धर।
मायर महलक लागिया याञो वल चलिया॥ ३२६
एइ कथा सुनिया ना थाकिल रैया॥ ३२७
एइ कथा वल गिया मयनार वरावर।
तैल परिच्छा दिवार चाय तोमार वरावर॥ ३२८
एइ कथा सुनिया मयना हासिते लागिल।
तोमार वुद्धि नय वधु सकलर चक्र।
यत वुद्धि सिखिया देय निरासी सकल॥ ३२९
एक परिच्छार वदल सात परिच्छा दिमु।
तवु तोर राजार वेटा वाड़ी घर छाड़ामु॥ ३३०

तोक वलों भाइया खेतु वाक्य मोर धर॥ ३३१
आताइला पाताइला चौका नेञो वल आरोपिया।
तिनटा नारिकोलर फल तेहिरा खिचिया॥ ३३२

३२२। परखिया = परीक्षा॥ ३२५। दुयार = द्वितीयेर॥ ३२९। निरासी = नीरस॥

साइट मेान काड़ाइ दिल चौकाय् चड़ाइया़ ।
आसी मेान तैल दिल काड़ाइत चड़ाइया़ ॥ ३३३
साल काष्ठे आगुन दिल सुलकाइया़ ।
उपरर छावनी मारिल तुलिया़ ॥ ३३४
सात दिन पर्य्यन्त जाल देय् निदम करिया़ ॥ ३३५
एक दिन दुइ दिन पञ्च दिन हइल ।
सात दिन अन्तरत छावनी उठाइल ॥ ३३६
तैल गरम हइया़छे आगुनर समान ।
एइ कथा जानाइल खेतु राजार बराबर ॥ ३३७
तैल परिच्छा हइल गोलाम बराबर ॥ ३३८
कि आज्ञा बलेन तुमि राज राजेस्वर ।
एइ कथा बल गिया़ मायर बराबर ॥ ३३९
तैल परिच्छा तैया़र हइल राजार बराबर ।
राजा तलब करे मा सीघ्र करे चल ॥ ३४०

तोर बापर खांओँ ना तोर राजार बापर खांओँ ।
तोमार ऊकुमत कि परिच्छा दिबार यांओँ ॥ ३४१

एइ कथा जानाइल राजार बराबर ॥ ३४२
एइ कथा सुनिया़ राजा क्रोद्धमान हइल ।
धरर सेंओया़ली गामछा राजा खेतुक फेलाइया़ दिल ॥ ३४३
ऐ गामछा दिया़ बान्धिल भिंड़िया़ ।
मय़ना मतिक दिल तैलत फेलाइया़ ॥ ३४४
येन मते मय़ना मति तैले पड़िल ।
धां धां करिया़ अनल सर्गत देखा दिल ॥ ३४५
तैलत पड़िया़ मय़ना डुबिल गला हइते ।
आञ्जले आञ्जले तैल मुकठिया़ बसाय् माथे ॥ ३४६
सम्भ्राट देखिया़ राजा क्रोद्धमान हइल ।
गोलाम गोलाम बलिये खेतुक ए गाली पाड़िल ॥ ३४७
उपरर छावनी मायर नओ तुलिया़ ।
नओ दिन भरिया़ जाल देओ निदम करिया़ ॥ ३४८

---

३४० । तैयार = طیار ॥

एक दिन दुइ दिन तिन दिन हइल ।
ओ रुप युइल मयना एकतर करिया ।
सरिसार रुप हइल काया वदलाइया ॥ ३४९
नओ दिन अन्तरत खेतु छावनी उठाइल ।
जननी ना देखिया खेतु कान्दिवार लागिल ॥ ३५०
एइ कथा जानाइल राजार वरावर ।
मा तोर करिया गेल यमर घर ॥ ३५१
कार जन्ये पागड़ि राखिछ मस्तकर उपर ।
आमाक छुइया जल ना खाय वामन पञ्च जन ॥ ३५२

मा मा वलिया राजा कान्दिवार लागिल । ३५३

विधि आमाक माछाड़ा करिल दीननाथ रे ।
एइ छिल कपालर लेखा ।
मायर सङ्गे ना हइल देखा ॥ धुया ॥ ३५४

एक मुट खोचा लइल हस्तत करिया ।
तैलर माझत वेड़ाय हास्तिया ॥ ३५५
एक हाल दुइ हाल तिन हाल हइल ।
तिन हालर समय गामछा उठाइल ॥
मद्दा मांस नाइ मयनार अनलर भितर ॥ ३५६
सोल मरदे नओ कड़ाइ साइङ्ग करिया ।
तेपथीत नि याया तैल फेलाइल ढालिया ॥ ३५७
धां धां करिया अनल सर्ग देखा दिल ।
सरिसार रुप हयया दुवाय नुकाइल ॥ ३५८
अकारने खेतु कान्दिवार लागिल ।
खेतुर कान्दने मयनार दया हइल ॥ ३५९

काइन्दना काइन्दना गोलाम खेतु कान्दन छेमा कर ।
मुइ मयना पोड़ा ना यांओं आगुनर भितर ॥ ३६०
साइट मोन कड़ाइ लइल हस्तत करिया ।
राजार अग्रे दिल हाजिर करिया ॥ ३६१

---

३५५ । मुट = मुष्टि ॥ ३५७ । मरदे = مرد (Nom. Plur.) ॥

एक एक करिया सात परिछा दिल ।
सात परिछाय् मयना उतरिया गेल ॥ ३६२

राजा बले सुन मयना मति मा तुंइ ।
तुइ ग्यान सिखिलु कोन सिद्धार ठांइ ॥ ३६३
मोक ग्यान सिखिवार कथो कोन आउलर ठांइ । ३६४
मुइ ग्यान सिखिनु गोरक नाथर ठांइ ।
तोक ग्यान सिखिवार कंथों खोला हाड़िर ठांइ ॥ ३६५
हाड़िर कथा सुनिया राजा कर्नंत दिल हात ।
अधर्म्म कथा आनिल जिह्वात ॥ ३६६
हाड़ि छाड़ जाति खेतखाना निकाइया ना करे खान ।
वाइस दण्ड राजा हइया करिमु हाड़िक प्रनाम ॥ ३६७

मयना बले सुन यादु चुप करिया कइस कथा ।
हाड़ि येन ना सुने अभिसाप दिले मरिवु एखन ॥ ३६८
तोर नगरिया प्रदीप जले तैले आर घिये ।
ए हाड़ि प्रदीप ज्वालाय् सुध गङ्गार जले ॥ ३६९
यत गुटि प्रदीप नाइ तोर नगरियार घरे ।
अत गुटि प्रदीप हाड़िर खपरार भितरे ॥ ३७०
काहार घरे खाय् हाड़ि काहार घरे याय् ।
मुखर जोओयावे दरिया वान्दा याय् ॥ ३७१
दरवारे थाकिया राजा वेचरित मन ।
दयार भाइ गोलाम खेतु डाके घने घन ॥ ३७२
कोथाय् गेल भाइ आगे पान खामु ।
वाप कालिया पण्डितक हाजिर करिमु ॥ ३७३

एइ कथा सुनिया खेतु ना थाकिल रैया ।
पण्डितर महलक लागिया गेल चलिया ॥ ३७४
तोक बलों पण्डित ठाकुर वाक्य मोर धर ।
राजा तलव करे महलर भितर ।
सीघ्रगति चलिया याओ राज दरवार ॥ ३७५

---

३६३ । ठांइ — (अधि)ष्ठाने (?) ॥

चटक धुति मठक धुति परिधान करिया ।
जोड़ जोड़ पैता दिले गलाय् तुलिया ॥ ३७६
पञ्जिकार दफ्तर लइल वगले डाविया ।
राज दरवारक लागिया चलिल छांटिया ॥ ३७७
भर काछारि राजा करे डाम्बा डौल ।
हेन समय् खाड़ा हइल पण्डितर कुमर ॥ ३७८
धर्म्मावतार वलिया प्रनाम जानाइल ।
कुलर देवता वलिया महाराज प्रनाम जानाइल ॥ ३७९
भाइया ठाकुर वलिया पालङ्कत वसाइल ।
ओ ठाकुर ओ ठाकुर दैवक चुड़ामनि ॥ ३८०
कोन दिना राजार वेटा सिलाइवे भुलि कांथा ।
कोन दिना राजार वेटा मुड़ाइवे माथा ॥ ३८१
कोन दिना महाराज भुसङ्ग माखिवे ।
कोन दिना धर्मी राज दुइ कर्न छेदिवे ॥ ३८२
कोन दिना धर्मी राज डोड़ कपिन पड़िवे ।
कोन दिना दिमु मोर हातत दोयादस ॥ ३८३
कोन दिना हवे आमार विदेस गमन ।
एइ गना गनिया देखो आमार वरावर ॥ ३८४
सुभ सुभ करिया पञ्जिका वाहेर करिल ।
आपनि सिद्धान्तर पञ्जिका वले आखो दिया ॥ ३८५

मङ्गलवारर दिन सिलाइवे भुलि कांथा ।
वुधवारर दिन मुड़ाइवे माथा ॥ ३८६
वृहस्पतिवारर दिन भुसङ्ग माखिवे ।
सुक्रवारर दिन राजा दुइ कर्न छेदिवे ॥ ३८७
सुक्रवारर दिन राजा दुइ कर्न छेदिवे ।
सनिवारर दिन राजा डोड़ कपिन पड़िवे ॥ ३८८
रविवार दिन राजा हातत दोयादस ।
ए दिवसे हवे राजा विदेस गमन ॥ ३८९
वाड़ी हइते निया यावे तोमाक वुद्धि भरसा दिया ।
किछु दुःख दिवे तोमाक जङ्गल वाड़ी दिया ।
आर किछु दुःख दिवे वाला वाड़ी दिया ॥ ३९०

---

३८५ । आखो = रव ॥

आर किछु दुःख दिवे श्रीकला नगरत ।
वान्दी थुइया खावे तोमाक ञ्चिरा वेस्यार घरत ॥ ३९१
वेस्यार परिधान हवे आगुन पाटर साड़ी ।
तोर राजार परिधान हवे वार गांइटे दड़ि ।
आकाड़ि धानर चाउल दिवे विचिया वार्त्तकि ॥ ३९२
विचिया वार्त्तकि दिवे पोड़ाइया खावा ।
एकेतो निदारुन वेस्या लवन तैल माना ॥ ३९३
वेस्या यावेन खेतखाना तुलिया धरवेन झाड़ि ।
चक्षु मञ्जिया येंगाइवेन वेस्यार वापेन पानि ॥ ३९४
प्रातेक उठिया माहरवे तोमाक वाखनर वाड़ी ।
पायर सइन्या उठाइवे पायर गना गन ॥ ३९५
सिकिया वाकुया दिवे दुइटा जलर झाड़ि ।
दिनठाय भोजन हवे वार भार पानि ॥ ३९६

राजा वले सुन ठाकुर दुख सुख कपालर लेखा ।
मऊत लिखा यांय विधाता लिखियाछे ।
आड़ाइ अक्षरे खण्डन यावार नय ॥ ३९७
कोथाय गेल भाइ खेतु आगेया पान खामु ।
दान दक्षिना दिया विदाय करिया दिमु ॥ ३९८
किछु दान दिया विदाय करिया दिल ।
वापर कालर नापितक आनिया हाजिर कर ॥ ३९९
नापितर महलक लागिया गेल चलिया ।
नापितक तवे आनिल डाकिया ।
भांइड़ क्षुर लइया आस चलिया ॥ ४००
भर काचारि राजा करे डाम्बा डौल ।
हेन काले खाड़ा हइल नापितर कुमर ॥ ४०१
येन मते धर्म्मि राजा नापितक देखिल ।
पाट हइते महाराजा मृत्तिकाय नामिल ।
नाट मन्दिर दालान कोटा भाङ्गिया गेल ॥ ४०२
गाछ कान्दे गाछानि कान्दे गाछर कान्दे पाता ।
वनर हरिनी कान्दे हेट करिया माथा ॥ ४०३

---

३९५ । सइन्या = शय्या ॥ ३९७ । मऊत = موت ॥ ४०२ । नाट = नृत्य ॥

घाटियालर घाटत कान्दे वाइस काहन नाओ ।
वाइस काहन नौका कान्दे तेइस काहन डांड़ि ।
तार माझतर कान्दे विसासर काण्डारि ॥ ४०४
हरिनर वालाखाना कान्दे कोकरान हाओखाना ।
कान्दे वेस्यार तालीम खाना ॥ ४०५
पिञ्जिरार माझत कान्दे टिटिया मञ्जर ।
सिकारि खेलाइते कान्दे नओ वुड़ि कुकुर ॥ ४०६
डाक्टरखाना तोसाखाना कान्दे ठांइ ठांइ ।
जलटङ्गि गोकुल कान्दे लेखा योखा नाइ ॥ ४०७
हातिसालाय हाति कान्दे पैघरत कान्दे घोड़ा ।
पाट महलर कान्दने भिजे जामा जोड़ा ॥ ४०८
एक सत गावि कान्दे गलाय नेज दिया ।
नओ वुड़ि कुत्ता कान्दे चरनत पड़िया ॥ ४०९
एक सत रानी कान्दे मृत्तिकाय गैड़ दिया ।
अदुना पदुना कान्दे दुइ चरन धरिया ॥ ४१०

हाय हाय स्वामिधन पालान छाड़िया ।
के आर पालिया नवे हते अन्न दिया ॥ ४११
राजार मा मयना कान्दे चक्षत पानि दिया ।
एक झाड़ि गङ्गार जल योगाइल आनिया ॥ ४१२
एक नेओयाइज पाता आनिल योगाइया ।
स्वर्नर वाटित लइल जल ढालिया ॥ ४१३
येन मते राजार माथाय तुलिया दिल जल ।
राज्य भोम सिंहासन करे टलमल ॥ ४१४
क्षुर धरिया नापितर वेटा चतुर्द्दिकत चाय ।
कार हुकुम ना पाय हाजामत वानाय ॥ ४१५
मयना वले नापितर वेटा कार पाने चाओ ।
मोर यादुर माथा कामाइते ना घिनाओ ।
हिरा दिया वान्धि दिमु मानिक दिमु चिन ॥ ४१६

---

४०४ । विसासर = विश्वेश्वर । ४०५ । तालीम खाना = تعليم خانة ॥ ४०७ । डाक्टर = Doctor ॥ ४०८ । हाति = हस्ती ॥ ४१४ । भोम = भूमि ॥

सकल चुल कामाइश्रो राइख वंम चुलि।
श्रवस्य उड़ाइवु छारिवु कोन्था भुलि॥ ४१७
क्षुर तुलिया एक सत दिन राजार केस मृत्तिकाय् पड़िल।
केसी गङ्गा हइया वहिवार लागिल॥ ४१८
तुरु तुरु करिया मयना ऊङ्कार छाड़िल।
खोल सत मुनि ऊङ्कारत नामिल॥ ४१९
पुस्परथे नामिल गोरक विद्याधर।
ढेकिवाहने नामिल नारद मुनिवर॥ ४२०
वासोयार पिठित नामिया गेल भोला महेस्वर।
धनुकवाने नामिया गेल श्रीरामलच्मन॥ ४२१
पांच भाइ पाण्डव नामिल ठांइ ठांइ।
कान काटा छाड़ि सिद्धा लेखा योखा नाइ॥ ४२२
घसिर धुला दिया वदन ढाकिल।
सम्भ्राट देखिया मयना कान्दिवार लागिल॥ ४२३

मायर दुइ नयनर तारा रे। आरे श्रो वाछा।
श्रामार केवा लइल रे॥ ॥ धुया॥ ४२४

नापितर हस्तर क्षुर लइल काड़िया।
ए क्षुर कानफाड़ार हस्त दिल तुलिया॥ ४२५
येन मते कानफाड़ा क्षुर हस्ते पाइल।
राम राम वलिया राजार दुइकर्ण फाड़िल॥ ४२६
फाठिकर कुण्डल राजाक पड़ाइल।
भगवान वस्त्र श्रानिया योगाइल॥ ४२७
पांच वैष्णव धरिया कपिन पड़ाइवार लागिल।
ए डोर कपिन राजाक पड़ाइल॥ ४२८
राम खिलिका गले तुलि दिल।
कादुर थाल हस्तत तुलि दिल॥ ४२९
भाङ्गा कोंथा भाङ्गा कपिन भाङ्गा वर्हिवास।
सवे मेलिया द्वारत श्राछे चैत्यन्यर दास॥ ४३०
श्रीचैतन्य नित्यानन्द श्रधिक राधे सिता।
श्रीगुरु वैष्णव वन्दल भागवत गिता॥ ४३१

४२७। फाठिकर = स्फटिकेर॥

भिक्षा वलिया राजार वेटा कान्दिवार लागिल।
हाति घोड़ा दण्ड छत्र गोलाम खेतु भिक्षा दिल।
ऐ भिक्षा गुरुर चरनत दिया परनाम करिल॥ ४३२

या या राजार वेटा तोमाक दिनु वर।
तिन कोन पिर्थिवि टलिया गेले ना याओ यमर घर॥ ४३३
येन मते धर्म्मि राजा वेना मुख हइल।
सर्गर मुनिगन सर्गत चलि गेल॥ ४३४
पांच लोटा जले मयना स्नानान करिया।
हांसिया निज घरत मयना सोन्दाइल गिया॥ ४३५
लड़ दिया एक भात पञ्चास व्यनुन रन्धन करिया।
स्वर्नर थालत अन्न दिले परसिया॥ ४३६
भिङ्गरर भाड़िर जल दिलेक ढालिया।
अन्न खाओ अन्न खाओ राज दुलालीया।
हांसिया खेलिया याओ परदेसक लागिया॥ ४३७

येन मते थालत अन्न देखिल।
कपालत मारिया चड़ कान्दिवार लागिल॥ ४३८
यखन आछिलाम मा राज्यत इस्वर।
स्वर्नर थालत अन्न खाइनु विस्तर॥ ४३९
एखन हइनु कोड़ाकर भिकारि।
स्वर्नर थालत अन्न खाइते ना पारि॥ ४४०
एक खान कलार पात आनिल काटिया।
ताहात अन्न गुटिक लइल ढालिया॥ ४४१
भाङ्गा तुम्वा आनिल धरिया।
ताहात जल फुटिक लइल ढालिया॥ ४४२
हातत मुखत जल दिया कोन काम करिल।
स्री कृष्ण वलिया अन्न मुखत तुलिया दिल।
एक गासे दुइ गासे पञ्च गास खाइल॥ ४४३
अन्न खाया जलर दिगत चाय।
भाङ्गा तुम्वा दिया जल उसिया पलाय॥ ४४४

---

४२६ । व्यनुन = व्यंजन ॥ ४४२ । गासे = ग्रास ॥

म्रत्तिकाय् मुख लागाइया जल चुम्बुक मारि खाइल ।
देविर भाइ सनि कपाल चड़िल ॥ ৪৪৫
सनि केतु राजार गर्भ वास करिल ।
सकल सरीर राजार मलिन पड़िल ॥ ৪৪৬
करुना करिया मयना कान्दिवार लागिल ॥ ৪৪৭

आमार पुत्र वड़ धन रे के रे मिलिया दिवे ॥ ॥ धुया ॥ ৪৪৮

परदेसे याइया परार पति वास ।
आगे खावे गिरिलोक पश्चात तश्चास ॥ ৪৪৯
अतित वैष्णव देखिया ना करिओ हेला ।
गड़ हया परनाम करेन यार गलत माला ॥ ৪৫০
सरिसाते सब दुवलाते छिन ।
तखने पावु परदेसर चिन ॥ ৪৫১

फुल गोटेक देखिया फुल ना फाड़िमु ।
पाखी गोटेक देखिया ढेल ना मारिमु ॥ ৪৫২
पर स्त्रीक देखिया हास्य ना करिमु ।
आगत मा दाय् दिया पश्चात भिक्षा लमु ॥ ৪৫৩
सोल काहन कड़ि दिल झोलङ्गाय् साजाइया ।
कड़ीर कथा ना कन तोर गुरुर वरावर ॥ ৪৫৪
छाइ भस्म करिया कड़िक पटामु ।
यमर घर द्वारिर पाछे गमन करिमु ॥ ৪৫৫

एक सत रानी गेल खेतुर वरावर ।
अदुना पदुना गेल आपनार महल ॥ ৪৫৬
वार जागाय् चौकि पहरा तेर जागाय् थाना ।
अतित वैष्णव यावार ए वाड़ी माना ॥ ৪৫৭
येन मते कन्या दुइटि मन्दीर सोन्दाइल ।
विन छोड़ाने धर्म्मर कपाट आपने लागिल ॥ ৪৫৮
पासा धरिया वसिल आछो ना करिया ॥ ৪৫৯
ये दिन हलर पासा पड़िवे आउलिया ।
ए दिन मोर स्वामी याइवे मरिया ॥ ৪৬০

राज्य भार रइल जननी मायर कोलत।
छाड़ि राजा चलिया गेल परदेस सहरत ॥ ৪৬১
एक क्रोस दुइ क्रोस पञ्च क्रोस गेल।
चरन फाटिया राजार रक्त पड़िवार लागिल ॥ ৪৬২

दुख मोर लिखियाछे कपाले ओरे विधि निरले वसिया ॥ धुया ॥ ৪৬৩

एक दिन दुइ दिन सात दिन हइल।
किवा रात्र किवा दिन हाटिवार लागिल ॥ ৪৬৪
एइ राजार मुलुक छाड़िया अन्य मुलुक गेल।
हारि वले जय विधि मोर कपालर फल ॥ ৪৬৫
दम्भ कथा वलिछे राजा आमार वरावर।
किछु दुख देँओँ घड़िकर भितर ॥ ৪৬৬
तुरु तुरु करिया छाड़ि ऊङ्कार छाड़िल।
सुन्नाकारत हारि सिद्धा जङ्गल सिर्ज्जाइल ॥ ৪৬৭
छोट जङ्गल छाड़िया वड़ जङ्गले पाओ।
आउ ढाउ सुखाइल मुखे ना आइसे आओ ॥ ৪৬৮
सुन्नाकारत हारि गेल सुन्नत चलिया।
दोनो हस्तत याय राजा जङ्गल ठेलिया ॥ ৪৬৯
इन्नि काटे विन्नि काटे रक्त पड़े धारे।
हाटिवार ना पारे राजा कपाल चड़ मारे ॥ ৪৭০

आमार एइ दुःख वैलमु कार आगे।
गुरु धन हइल निदारुन ॥ ॥ धुया ॥ ৪৭১

आर किछु दुःख दिल वाला वाड़ी दिया।
राजार कान्दनत छाड़िर दया उवजील।
केल कदम्बर गाछ घांटाय सिर्जाइल ॥ ৪৭২
वृक्ष तलत याय राजा सहरत गोविन।
आंजुलत आंजुलत चक्षत आइल निन ॥ ৪৭৩
जल भाङ्गिया वाला भाङ्गिया वड़ पेनु दुःख।
वांओ उरु मृत्तिकाय देओ अनेक मारि सुख ॥ ৪৭৪

৪৬৭। सुन्नाकारत = शून्याकाशे ॥ ৪৭২। उवजील = उपजिल अर्थात् जन्म हइल ॥
৪৭৩। निन = निद्रा ॥ ৪৭৪। नु = पाइलाम ॥

वांञो उरु हारि म्त्तिकाय् फेलि दिल ।
सितान दिया राजा निद्राय् पड़िल ॥ ४७५
तुरु तुरु करिया हारि ऊङ्गार छाड़िल ।
एक सत यम डाकिया आनिल ॥ ४७६

हारि वले यम वाक्य मोर धर ।
सात हात ओसार माछि एक वुक उच ।
ऐटे हइत वान्धि नि याओ दारियापुर सहर ॥ ४७७
एं कथा सुनिया यम ना थाकिल रैया ।
माछि वान्धिते यम गेल चलिया ॥ ४७८
सात हात ओसार माछि एक वुक उच ।
ऐटे हइते वान्धि नि याइल दारियापुर सहर ॥ ४७९
हनुमान वलिया ऊङ्गार छाड़िल ।
किकु किकु वच्च माड़ाल लागाइल ॥ ४८०
वच्च चापर राजाके तुलिया मारिल ।
गुरु गुरु वलिया राजा कान्दिया उठिल ॥ ४८१
माछि वान्धिया आमि वड़ पेनु दुख ।
वार कड़ा कड़ि देओ खांओं सुख ॥ ४८२
वार कड़ार गाञ्जा खांओं किनिया ।
तवे तोमाक लइया याइ घाड़पुरक लागाइया ॥ ४८३
येन मते धर्म्मि राजा सम्वाद सुनिल ।
राम राम वलिया कर्नत हात दिल ॥ ४८४
ए गुलाक खान गुरु वाप मोँ ना जानों ।
एमन अनाचारर सङ्गत आइसे कोन जन ।
अनाचारर सङ्गत आइले अवस्य मरन ॥ ४८५
वार कड़ार वदलत गुरु वारो कान्ओन लओ ।
वान्दा छान्दार कार्य्य नाइ फिरिया घरे याओ ॥ ४८६
ध्यानत आछिल हाड़ि चमकिया उठिल ॥ ४८७
ध्यानत हाड़ि गुरु ध्यान करि चाय् ।
ध्यानर माझत सोल कान्ओन कड़ी झोलार लागाल पाय् ॥ ४८८
एर मा मान आके ज्ञानत डाङ्गर ।
सोल काहन कड़ि दिके झोलङ्गार भितर ॥ ४८९

---

४८२ । सुक = सुख ॥

तुख तुख करि हाड़ी ऊङ्कार छाड़िल ।
सेाल काञोन कड़ी सुन्नत उड़ा उड़ाइया दिल ॥ ४९०
आद मेान करिया एक मेान पाथर झोलाय सिर्जाइल ।
भात धरिया धर्म्मि राजा डुगिवार लागिल ॥ ४९१
दे दे कड़ि वलिया हाड़ि काउसिवार लागिल ।
एकवार दुइवार गोस्या नागाइल पाइल ॥ ४९२
झोलङ्कार गिरा खुलिया फेलाइल ।
झोलार गिर खुलिया पड़िया गेल धान्दा ।
झोलार कड़ि झोलाय नाइ अचम्बितेर कथा ॥ ४९३

नयान कोन नाचे ।
ना जानि कपाले किवा आछे ॥ ॥ धुया ॥ ४९४

केने केने गुरु वाप अधर्म्मे छाड़ दया ।
झोलेर कड़ि झोलात नाइ कमवक्ताक राख वान्दा ॥ ४९५

चट करि साच्ची थुइल हाड़ि वसु माता माइ ।
तोमरा एञो साच्ची ।
आपना आपनि वान्दा निछे हाड़िञो ना राखि ॥ ४९६

धर्म्मि राजाक लइल झोलाय भड़िया ।
दारियापुर सहरत गेल चलिया ॥ ४९७
वान्दा नेञो वान्दा नेञो गोयालीनी माइ ।
वार कड़ा कड़ि थाकिया वान्दा थुइवार चाइ ।
वार कड़ा कड़ि पाइले गाञ्जा खाइवार चाइ ॥ ४९८
देखि देखि केमन चेला देखिवार चाइ ॥ ४९९
हात कोना धरिया राजाक वेइर कैल टानिया ।
झलमल करिया राजा उठिल जलिया ॥ ५००
गोयालिनी वले गुरु करि निवेदन ।
सुन्दर रुप देखि राजाक भातर उपर ।
एञो नाकि खावार पारे गोयाल लोकर घर ॥ ५०१

---

४९० । सुन्नत = ख़ून्चे ॥ ४९२ । गोस्या = غصه ॥ ४९५ । कमवक्ताक = كمبخت كو ॥ ५०१ । नाकि = न्याय् ॥

काड़िया भरिया टाका देओ झोला भरिया नेओ ।
आमार महल छाड़िया अन्य महल याओ ॥ ५०२
महाराजाक लइले तवे हस्तत धरिया ।
दोकानर गलि वेड़ाय् हांटिया ॥ ५०३
वान्दा नेओ वान्दा नेओ चिड़ा वेचि माइ ।
येन मते चिड़ा वेचि राजाक देखिल ।
चिड़ार दोकान खान पाकेया फेलिल ॥ ५०४
राजार कमर धल्ये मरों वलिया ।
अनेक करिया निल छोड़ाइया ॥ ५०५
वान्दा नेओ वान्दा नेओ हलदि वेचि माइ ।
वान्दा नेओ वान्दा नेओ साक वेचि माइ ॥ ५०६
वान्दा नेओ वान्दा नेओ आड़इ वेचि माइ ।
वान्दा नेओ वान्दा नेओ कालाइ वेचि माइ ॥ ५०७
येन मते कालाइ वेचि राजाक देखिल ।
घरर स्वामिक आइल वाप दाय् दिया ॥ ५०८
येत दोकान सव फेलाइल पाकेया ।
राजार कमर धरिल मरिनु वलिया ॥ ५०९
चिड़ा वेचि उठिया वले काला वेचि ऊत्तिया तुइ ।
छाड़िया दे राजार कमर आरो धरनु मुइ ॥ ५१०
राजार कमर धरिया टानिवार लागिल ।
अकारन करिया राजा कान्दिवार लागिल ॥ ५११
राजार कान्दने छाड़िर दया जनमिल ।
इन्द्र राजाक लागिया ऊङ्कार छाड़िल ॥ ५१२
धुम धाम करिया पाथर पड़िते लागिल ।
राजार कमर छाड़िया सव घराघरि गेल ॥ ५१३
दुयार छाड़ दुयार छाड़ कालाइ वेचि भोन ।
भिजिया वाहेरा देखन भिजिया मरि वाहेरा देखन ॥ ५१४
येन मते कालाइ वेचि सेलटा कथा पाइल ।
छाउक दाउक करिया दरजा छाड़ि दिल ॥ ५१५
कालाइ काड़ा गाइन निया ये आइल ।
ये गाइन दिया डाङ्गावार लागिल ॥ ५१६
नाक चुल काटिया टेराडारा दिल ।
घारत हात दिया वाहिर करि दिल ॥ ५१७

ओक काड़िया गमन विजय हालुया ।
साच्चात उतरिल याइया ॥ ५१८
वान्दा नेओ वान्दा नेओ हालुयार घर ।
सुन्दर चेला वान्दा थोंओं तोर हालुयार घर ॥ ५१९
सुन्दर रुप देखों भाखड़ उपर ।
एओ नाकि खावार पारे चासा लोकर घर ॥ ५२०
इहार योग्यवान आछे हिरा वेस्यार घर ।
केमन करि यावेन नटिर महलर भितर ॥ ५२१
योड़् योड़् दामरा थुइचे दरओयाजा टाङ्गिया ।
कोन भितकार राजा आइसे महले चलिया ॥ ५२२
एक डाङ्ग यदि मारे दामराय तुलिया ।
एक हाजार टाका नेय दरओयाजाय वसिया ॥ ५२३
ओक काड़िया विजय गमन ।
नटिर वाङ्गलाय याइया दिल दरिसन ॥ ५२४
लकड़ि खुलिया एक डाङ्ग डाङ्गाइल ।
सब्द हइल नटिर पुरि वार्त्ता जानाइल ॥ ५२५

वान्दि वान्दि वलिया डाकाइवार लागिल ।
कोटेकार महाराजा चलिया आसिल ॥
ताहाके आन तुमि चाम्बर हाकाइया ॥ ५२६
एइ कथा सुनिया वान्दि ना थाकिल रया ।
हाड़िर साच्चात गेल चलिया ॥ ५२७
केने२ गुरुधन एत दुर गमन ।
सिंहासन थाकिते केन मृत्तिकाय सयन ॥ ५२८
वासा खोड़ा नाइ आमार भोलार भितर ।
एकना चेला आछे भोलाङ्गार भितर ॥ ५२९
वार कड़ा कड़ि थाकिया वान्दा थुइवार चाइ ।
वार कड़ा कड़ि पाइले गांजा किनिया खाइ ॥ ५३०
वान्दा नाकि निवे तोमार हिरा नटि माइ ।
देखों देखों केमन चेला देखिवारे चाइ ॥ ५३१
हात कोना धरिया वेर करिल टानिया ।
ढल मल करिया राजा उठिल ज्वलिया ॥ ५३२

रुप देखिले नयान भोरे। ॥ धुया ॥ ५३३

एइ कथा जानाइल वान्दि नटिर वरावर।
येमन रुप आछे राजार चरनर उपर॥
सेमन रुप नाइ तोमार मुखर उपर॥ ५३४
ये राजा वलिया तर्प्प कर ए वार वत्सर।
सेइ राजार नागाल पाइलु दरजार उपर॥ ५३५
एइ कथा सुनिया नटि न थाकिल रैया।
राजार साछात चलिल छांटिया॥ ५३६

छाड़ि वले सुन नटि आमार वरावर।
भाल चेला वान्दा थुइ तोमार वरावर॥ ५३७
वार कड़ा कड़ि थाकिया वान्दा थुइवार चाइ।
वार कड़ा कड़ि पाइले गांजा किनिया खाइ॥ ५३८
एइ कथा सुनिया नटि न थाकिल रैया।
वन्दरर साउद महाजनक आनिल डाकिया॥ ५३९
दोयात खत कलम योगाइल आनिया।
वार कड़ा कड़ि नटि आनिल गनिया॥ ५४०
लेख लेख वलिया छाड़ि हुकुम भाला दिल।
सन तारिख सौ कागजत लिखिल॥ ५४१
हिरा नटि नामटा कागजत लिखिल।
ए वार कड़ा कड़ि कागजत लिखिल॥ ५४२
धर्म्मर नामटा कागजत लिखिल।
ए कलम फेलाइया दिल छाड़िर वरावर॥ ५४३
येन मते छाड़ि सिद्धा हस्तत कलम पाइल।
राम राम करिया दस्तखत करिया दिल॥ ५४४
वार कड़ा कड़ि गनिया छाड़िर हस्तत दिल।
छाड़िर हस्तत महाराजाक नटीर हस्तत दिल॥ ५४५
ए दिन हइते धर्म्मि राजा वन्धन पड़िल।
ए खत तुलिया नटीर हस्तत दिल॥ ५४६
काम क्रोध मनि भिड़िया वान्धिल।
ना राखी ना पुरुस राजाक करिल॥ ५४७

येन मते हिरा नटी वेना मुख हइल।
ए वार कड़ा कड़ी म्रत्तिकाय् गाड़िल॥ ५४८
येन मत धर्म्मि राजा वेना मुख हइल।
सुनाली कुमड़ा हइये पाताल भेजिल॥ ५४९
चौद्द ताल जलर भितर येाग आसन धरिल।
वार वतसर थाकिल छाड़ि ध्यान धरिया॥ ५५०
येन मते धर्म्मि राजा फिरिया देखिल।
गुरुक ना देखिया राजा कान्दिवार लागिल॥ ५५१

नटी वले राजार वेटा कान्द कि कारन।
तोमार वादे तप करि ए वार वत्सर॥ ५५२
कोन्टि गेल वान्दि आगेया पान खाव।
धर्म्मि राजाक स्नान छिनान कराइया।
येटे ये सोभा पाय् आन राजाक पराइया॥ ५५३
छिनान कराइया आनिल धरिया।
विछान करिते नटी भाल जाने॥ ५५४
साटीर उपर पाटो विछाय् एक वुक उछल।
तार उपर फेलेया दिल इन्द्र कम्वल॥ ५५५
लं जायफल करपुर राखिल ठांइ ठांइ।
दिप फेलाइवे राजा लेखा येाखा नाइ॥ ५५६
येन धर्म्मि राजा दुयारत पाओ दिल।
कोलात करिया राजाक विछानाय् वसाइल।
पानर वाटा दिल हाजिर करिया॥ ५५७
पान खिलि खाओ हे राजा गुया खानि खाओ।
ए अभागिनी नटी आमि माथा तुलिया चाओ॥ ५५८
लं जायफल कर्पुर देखिया मने हइल खुसि।
एकेक वेला तुलिया दिल खिलि चारि पांचि॥ ५५९
एक ठासन दुइ ठासन तिन ठासन दिल।
माओ ये करिछे वाधा मनत पड़िल॥ ५६०
परदेस याइया यादु पड़ाओ वह्विर्व्वास।
आगत खाइवे गिरिलोक पश्चात तल्लास॥ ५६१
अतित वैष्णव देखिया ना करिओ हेला।
गड़ हये परनाम जानान यार गलत माला॥ ५६२

फुल गोटेक देखिया फुल ना पाड़िवु ।
पाखि गोटेक देखिया डिमा ना मारिवु ॥ ५६३
परार स्त्री देखिया हास्य ना करिवु ॥ ५६४
सरिसाते सब दुबलाते हिन ।
तखने पावु परदेसर चिन ॥ ५६५
माएर कथा येन राजार मनत पड़िल ।
राम राम वलिया पानर खिलि ढालिया फेलाइल ॥ ५६६
ऐटे हइते नटीर मन खापा हइये गेल ।
केने २ पान ना खाओ राज राज्येश्वर ।
तोर गुने तप करि ए बार वत्सर ॥ ५६७
आपना हइते लइल पांचटा खिलि हस्तत करिया ।
धार्म्मिक राजार मुखत दिल तुलिया ॥
थुथु करिया पानर खिली फेलाइल ढालिया ॥ ५६८
येत्के धर्म्मि राजा सहरे सहरे वैसे ।
तेत्के हिरा नटी गाओ घिसिया वैसे ॥ ५६९
सार चन्दन रक्त चन्दन राजाक छिटिवार लागिल ।
मामा करिया राजा नटीक डाकिवार लागिल ।
यु याय ना यु याय ना राजा माओ वलिवार ॥ ५७०
राजार हस्त तुलिया नटी हृदत तुलिया दिल ।
मामा वलिया राजा दुग्ध खावार गेल ॥ ५७१
एकवार दुइवार राजा गोस्या नागाल पाइल ।
गोटा चारिक नटीर वाखान वलिवार नागिल ॥ ५७२

तोमार सनर कथा काइ ।
एमन पिरिती भाल नय ॥
जलाइया मनर वाति ।
जागिया पोहाइले राति ॥
रामे दिल दान ।
कुवुजा कि राधार समान ॥ ॥ धुया ॥ ५७३

किवा नटी नेहालेओ पाझाय २ चुल ।
नापितेर वली देखों येन धुतुरार फुल ॥ ५७४

---

५६७ । खापा = خفه ॥ ५७२ । गोस्या = غصه ॥

तोर नटीर व्यभार देखों खेओया घाटर नाओ।
घाटत कड़ि दिया आदमि हय पार।
एइ मत देखि नटी तोर कारेर व्यभार॥ ५७५
तोर नटी रुप देखों येन अन्ध कुप।
छाड़ि डोमे कुइया वावने पाड़े डुव॥ ५७६
चारि पहर गेल नटी वखाल करिया।
ताहातेओ डाकाय धर्म्मि राजा नटिक माओ वलिया॥ ५७७
एकवार दुइवार नटी गोस्था नागाइल।
पालङ्क हइते धर्म्मि राजाक गुड़ाइया फेलाइल॥ ५७८
वान्दी वान्दी वलिया नटी डाकिवार लागिल।
घाड़त हस्त दिया राजाक वाहेर करिया दिल॥ ५७९
नटीर परिधान हइल आगुन पाटर साड़ी।
धर्म्मि राजार परिधान हइल वार गाटिया धरि॥ ५८०
आकारि धानर चाउल दिले विचिया वार्त्तकि।
विचिया वार्त्तकि दिले पुरिया खाइवार साना।
एकें तो निदारुन नटो लवन तैल माना॥ ५८१
माघ मासिया जारे दिले वुड़ा एक खान साड़ी।
थाकिवार घर दिले छागलर खुपुड़ि॥ ५८२
सिकिया वाकुया दिले दुइटा जलर हाड़ि।
दिनटात भोजन करिले वार भार पानि॥ ५८३
वार भार पानिर माझत एक भार कमि पाय।
जल भारर वदली सात जने किलाय॥ ५८४
सिकिया वाकुया निले दुइटा जलर हाड़ि।
जल भरिवार गेल करतोया नदी॥ ५८५
एक भार दुइ भार तिन भार डुवाइल।
दिनटात महाराज वार भार उभाइल॥ ५८६
सात भाड़ुया धल्ले राजाक चित्ति करिया।
सोनाली खड़म नटी चरनत नागाइया॥ ५८७
राजार वुकत चड़िल ठसक मारिया।
छिनान करे हिरा नटी हासिया खेलिया॥ ५८८
छिनान करिया अङ्गे हइल यति।
भिजा वस्त्र फेलाइया पिन्दे सुकाला पाटर सारि॥ ५८९

५७५। व्यभार = व्यवहार॥ ५८९। यति = द्युति।

भिजा वस्त्र चिपिया दिले ये राजा मुख स्नागर उपर।
मुख धरिया कान्दे राजा वेलार दुइ पहर।
धाड़त हस्त दिया राजाक वाहेर कैरे दिल॥ ५९०
आजि कालि करिया वार वत्सर हइल॥ ५९१
सिकिया वाकुया निले दुइटा जवर छांड़ि।
जल भरिवार गेल करतोया नदी॥ ५९२
नदीर पाड़े याया राजा पड़िया गेल धान्दा।
अदुना पदुनार कथा ना सुनिल कानत।
परान हारावार आइलाम वुड़ा मार वचनत॥ ५९३

येन मत धर्म्मि राजा कन्यार नाम लैल।
उयटे हातर पसार आउलीया पड़िल।
अकारन करिया कन्या कान्दिवार लागिल॥ ५९४
वार वत्सर गेल स्वामि आस्रो ना करिया।
तेर वत्सर भाल हइल आसिया॥ ५९५
आजि केन हस्तर पसार पड़िल आउलीया।
ना जानि सोयामी धन गेल मरिया॥ ५९६

दुति गो कि मते वाहिर हमु।
दुखर कथा काइल सकालत निरलत कमु॥
वृन्दावनत वाजे वांसि।
मने कय स्यामक देखों आसि॥ ॥ धुया॥ ५९७

दोनो वइने रोदन करे नाट मन्दिर घरत।
सारी सुया पाखी सुनिल पिञ्जिरार माझात॥ ५९८
सारी उठिया वले सुया वड़ भाइ।
मा केन रोदन करे चल देखवार याइ॥ ५९९
जोरा जोरि करि पिञ्जिरार खाटी फेलिल भाङ्गिया।
ये दिया सारी सुया गेल उड़ाओ दिया॥ ६००
चालर खेड़ निचिया कन्यार वाजुत पड़े।
कोने २ माओ रोदन कर नाट मन्दिर घरे॥ ६०१
कन्या वले सुन वाछा पक्षि सकल।
वार वत्सर गेल तोर वावा राओदा करिया।
तेर वत्सर भार पाइल ना आइल फिरिया॥ ६०२

६०२। राओदा = ४७०१॥

আইজ কেনে মোর হস্তর পসার পড়িল আউলীয়া।
না জানি তোর পিতা গেল মরিয়া॥ ৫০৩
আমার দুই ভাইক দেখো মা ছাড়িয়া।
কোনটে আছে আমার পিতা আসি তল্লাস করিয়া॥ ৫০৪
যাও ২ বাবা পরদেস লাগিয়া।
কোটে আছে তোমার পিতা আইস তলাস করিয়া॥ ৫০৫
জননীর চরনত পাখী পরনাম করিল।
দক্ষিন পাঠনে পাখী উড়াও দিয়া গেল॥ ৫০৬
সাত দিন ভরি পাখী উড়িতে লাগিল।
তাতেও ধর্ম্মি রাজার লাগাল না পাইল॥ ৫০৭
নদীর পাড়ত আছে বট আর পাইকড়।
বটর ঠালত পাখী পইল উড়াও দিয়া॥ ৫০৮
পশ্চিম ঠাল হইতে পাখী পুর্ব্ব ঠাল যায়।
ভার ধরি ধর্ম্মি রাজা জল ভরিবার যায়॥ ৫০৯
জলত নামিয়া দন্ত মাজ্জিবার লাগিল।
মাথার উপর পাখি রাজার উড়িবার লাগিল॥ ৫১০

তোরা নাকিন হন রাজা গোপী চন্দ্র।
তোমার খবরত আসি ভাই দুই জন॥ ৫১১
হস্ত বাড়েয়া দিল।
উড়াও দিয়া পাখী দুইটা বাজুত পড়িল॥ ৫১২
দুই নয়নে প্রেম ধারা রাজা বহিবার লাগিল।
যত দুক্ষ হইয়াছে রাজার বলিবার লাগিল॥ ৫১৩
নাকিড়ি পাকিড়ি পাত আনিলেন ছিড়িয়া।
দাঁত দিয়া খাগড়ার কলম মাঠাইলে বসিয়া॥ ৫১৪
কাঞ্ছী অঙ্গুলী দিয়া বাঁও উড়াত ফাড়িল।
এ রক্ত দিয়া লেখন লিখিবার লাগিল।
যত দুক্ষার কথা রাজা লিখিবার লাগিল॥ ৫১৫
সুমাও হইলে নিবেন উদ্ধার করিয়া।
কুমাও হইলে থুইবেন পাপত ফেলিয়া॥
এই লিখন দিস তোর বরাইর বরাবর॥ ৫১৬
রাজার চরনত পাখি প্রনাম জানাইয়া।
ময়নার মহলত পাখি গেল উড়াও দিয়া॥ ৫১৭

चाल छेन्दा करिया लेखन दिल फेलाइया ।
देख देख रे वुड़ा साली तोर मुख्ख खान पड़िया ॥ ६१८
सुमाञो हइले निवे उद्धार करिया ॥ ६१९
खाम खुलिया लेखन पड़िवार लागिल ।
अकारन करिया पाखि कान्दिवार लागिल ॥ ६२०

वियाने गियाछे यादुरे ।
रविर भालाय् मैछ आमार वाछारे ॥ ॥ धुया ॥ ६२१

ध्यानत मयना वुड़ी ध्यान करि चाय् ।
चौद्द ताल जलर भितर हाड़िर लागाल पाय् ॥ ६२२
खखपा ज्ञान माइछे तुलिया ।
धाक भांय् हाड़ि सिद्धार फेलाइल काटिया ॥ ६२३
सरदि सागर दिया याछे भासिया ।
चुल जोड़ा धरिया मयना डाङ्गात उठाइल ॥ ६२४
वज्जर चापड़ हाड़िक कसिया मारिल ।
ध्यानत आछिल हाड़ि चमकिया उठिल ॥ ६२५
ध्यानत हाड़ी गुरु ध्यान करि चाय् ।
ध्यानर माझात मयनार लागाल पाय् ॥ ६२६
याँओं याँओं दिदि राजाक लागिया ।
तोर वेटाक उद्धार करिले पिछे खामु गाञ्जा ॥ ६२७
यदि काले छाइलार ज्ञान अल्प देखिव ।
छाइ भस्म करिया हाड़ि तोक यम घर पाठाव ॥ ६२८
ये घाटत राजार वेटा जल भरे वसिया ।
ए घाटत हाड़ि सिद्धा राजा उत्तरिल याया ॥ ६२९
दुर हइते देखिल राजा हाड़िर चकर ।
दुइटा हाड़ि धुइले दुइटे भाङ्गिया ॥ ६३०
माधार चुल राजा दुइ अर्द्ध करिल ।
हाड़िर चरनत राजा पड़िल भजिया ॥ ६३१
ए धर्म्मि राजाक भोलङ्गाय् भड़िया ।
नटीर महलत गेल चलिया ॥ ६३२
नटीर महलत याया हाड़ि ऊङ्गार छाड़िल ।
दुम दुम करि पुरि नड़िवार लागिल ॥ ६३३
नटी वले वान्दी वेटि कार घाने चाओ ।

कोनटे कार अथीत आइछे विदाय् करि दाओ ॥ ६३४
एइ कथा सुनिया बान्दी आइल चलिया ।
हाड़िक देखिया बान्दी गेल फिरिया ॥ ६३५
एइ कथा जानाइल नटीर बराबर ।
अथीत नोआ हाड़ि लङ्केश्वर ॥ ६३६
एइ कथा सुनिया नटी कोन काम करिल ।
घरर भितर नटो लुकिया रहिल ॥ ६३७
नटी नुकाइया रइल मने आर मने ।
हाड़ि सिद्धा जानिते पाइल अन्तर ध्याने ॥
हातर आसा नड़ि मारिल तुलिया ॥ ६३८
तोक बलों आसा नड़ि वाक्य मोर धर ।
हात गलत बान्धिया हिरा नटिक हाजिर कर ॥ ६३९
एक आज्ञा पाइले सहस्र आज्ञा पाइल ।
गर्ज्जिया हिरा नटीर महलत सोन्दाइल ॥ ६४०
ढेकाइते २ नटि बाहर करे आनिल ।
बार कड़ा कड़ि हाड़ी तखन उठाइल ॥ ६४१
बार वत्सरिया खत नटी आनिया योगाइल ।
बार कड़ा कड़ी गनिया नटीर हातत दिल ॥ ६४२
नटीर हातर खत खान हाड़ीर हातत दिल ।
राम २ बलिया खत फाड़िया फेलाइल ॥ ६४३
एक हिड़ा गङ्गार जल हाड़ी आनिल योगाइया ।
सात भड़ुया धरिल नटीक चितर करिया ॥ ६४४
बाइस मोनिया खड़्ग राजार चरनत लागाइया ।
नटीर बुकत राजाक दिल चड़ाइया ॥ ६४५
येतके हैले नड़े आर चड़े ।
बर्त्तिस पाञ्जर नटीर भाङ्गी गुड़ा करे ॥ ६४६
राम २ बलिया येन जल मस्तकत ढाली दिल ।
यत किछु पाप गुना दुरे चलिया गेल ॥ ६४७
छिनान करिया राजा अद्भुत हइल यति ।
भिजा वस्त्र फेलाया पिन्दे सुकना पाटर धुति ॥ ६४८
हाड़ी बले राजार बेटा वाक्य मोर धर ।
बारो वत्सर तप करे नटी महलर भितर ।
किछु वाक्य सिद्ध कर नटीर बराबर ॥ ६४९

या या हिरा नटी तोक दिनु वर ।
वगदुल पाखि हइया थाक राज्यर भितर ॥ ६५०
मनि वाक्य कथा ना हइल ।
वगदुल रूप हइये सर्गत उड़े गेल ॥ ६५१
वाम हस्त दिया नटीक धरिल ।
नटीक धरिया दुइ खान करिल ॥ ६५२
आग धर दिले सर्गत उड़ाइया ।
पाछ धर दिल दरियात फेलाइया ॥ ६५३
दरियात पड़िया नटी दोहाइ फिराइल ॥ ६५४
या या नटी तोक दिनु वर ।
चेका माछ हइया थाक जलर भितर । ६५५
या या चामाइ वान्दी तोक दिनु वर ।
वेस्या हइया थाक राज्यर भितर ॥ ६५६
जुयान कालत खाओ कामाइ करिया ।
सेस कालत धरेक पाइक भातार ।
ऊलिया गुड़िया भाङ्गिवे तोर वत्रिस पाञ्जर ॥ ६५७
या या हिरा धन काड़ी तोक दिनु वर ।
खोलाछाटि हइया थाक खोलाछाटि सहर ॥ ६५८

हिरार वाड़ी घर नख भख करिया ।
ज्ञान सिखिवार राजाक लइ गेल धरिया ॥ ६५९
तोक वलों राजार वेटा वाक्य मोर धर ।
किछु भिक्षा करि आन वन्दरर भितर ।
सिस्य गुरु वान्धि खाइ परदा सहर ॥ ६६०
शमित राजार वेटा नामे ब्रह्मचारि ।
केमन करे भिक्षा करे निश्चय ना जानि ॥ ६६१
गोटा चारिक कथा यखन राजाक सिखाइल ।
हाते पात्र निया गमन करिल ॥ ६६२
छाड़ी वले जयरे विधि मोर कर्म्मर फल ।
मोर घरर चेला कोना सर्व्वाङ्ग सुन्दर ।
गिरिर घरर वउ वेटीक करिवे पागल ॥ ६६३

---

६६३ । वउ = वधू ॥

नेङ्गडी कोटओयाल हइल मुरत वदलाइया।
घर घर ऊड़का आसिल लागाइया॥ ६६४
हायान भायान हिलाल कुकुर।
भिक सिक ना पाइया यावे हाड़ीर हजुर॥ ६६५
भिक्षा वलिया राजा गमन करिल।
तुर तुर करि हाड़ी ऊङ्कार काड़िल॥ ६६६
सर्ग हइते पांच कन्या ऊङ्कारे नामाइल।
पांच थाल अन्य आनिया येगाइल॥ ६६७
आपना अंसर अन्न खाइल।
राजार भागर अन्न यतने राखिल।
आड़ाइ पुटि छान अन्नत छाड़ि दिल॥ ६६८
थुक घाङ्गार अन्नक थुइल माखिया।
मोड़ा मिसरि रस दिया थुइल माखिया॥ ६६९
साइल केल्ला दुरा थुइल ढाकिया।
भिक्षा रुप धर्म्मि राजा वेड़ाय् चेंचाइया॥ ६७०
हापरे भापरे राजाक हिलाय् कुकुर।
भिक सिक ना पाइया गेल हाड़ीर ऊजुर॥ ६७१
गुरु धन तोर देसर लोक देखिनु निदय् निठुर।
भिक सिक ना देय् हिलाय् कुकुर॥ ६७२
नाइ पाइस ना पाइस भिक्षा वेटा मोर सेवा नाइलया।
एकना सतीर नागाल पानु पथे वसिया॥ ६७३
तांय् गुटिक अन्न दिया गेइल आसिया।
आपनकार अंसर अन्न खाइल वसिया।
तोर भागर अन्न थुचि यतने करिया॥ ६७४
ढुलिते पड़िते राजा अन्नर काछत गेल।
अन्न देखिया कपालत चड़ दिल॥ ६७५
एमन अन्न ना खाय् आमार कुत्ता सकल।
सेइ अन्नर नागाल पानु राज राजेश्वर॥ ६७६
तुर तुर करिया हाड़ि ऊङ्कार काड़िल।
वार वत्सर खिदा सरीरत नागाइल॥ ६७७
छि छि खिन २ करिया एक ग्रास खाइल।
अम्रत मिठा राजा मुखत लागिल॥ ६७८
फिर एकना गासर वेला हात कोना धरिल।

कड़ा काड़ी करिया आड़ाइ गास खाइल।
आड़ाइ पुटी ज्ञान तखनइ सिखिल ॥ ६७९
ज्ञाने ध्यानत वान्दि दिल ऊली।
गोदा यमर मायर सङ्गत कैल कोलाकोली ॥ ६८०
ज्ञाने ध्यानत वान्दि दिल घुड़ा।
गोदा यमक करिया दिल खोंड़ा ॥ ६८१
तुल तुल करिया छाड़ी ऊङ्कार छाड़िल।
वाड़ीर कथा वार्त्ता राजार मनत पड़िल ॥ ६८२
विदाय देओ २ गुरु धरम तरि।
आलक रथे देखि आसि घर छिरि वाड़ी ॥ ६८३
हातर आस तुलिया दिल राजार हातर उपर।
छाड़ीर चरनत राजा परनाम जानाइल ॥ ६८४
आसी मेानी आसा लइल घाड़त करिया।
रास्ता दिया चलिया याय राजा दुलालीया ॥ ६८५
छाड़ी सिद्धा हासे खल खल करिया।
अक छाड़ीया राजा नियाय गमन ॥ ६८६
आपनकार मङ्गलत गिया मेल चलिया।
तुल तुल करिया राजा सिंनाद वाजाय।
निन्दत आछिल कन्या चेतन हया याय ॥ ६८७
विन खड़ी दाम्मा घड़ि वाजिवार लागिल।
विन आगुन दुग्ध चाउल उथलीया पड़िल ॥ ६८८
हाटि २ प्रदीप जलिवार लागिल।
सरदि सागरत राजा वहिवार लागिल ॥ ६८९
चौद्दखान मधुकर भासिया उठिल।
श्री वृन्दावन राजा मुख लस हइल।
गर्भवति नारी सव प्रसव हइल ॥ ६९०

अथीत आइल रे।
आमार दरजार माझा रे ॥ ॥ धुया ॥ ६९१

कोनटे गेल वान्दी आगेया पान खामु।
कोनटेकार अथीत आइके विदाय करि दिमु ॥ ६९२

६८३। आलक = आलोक ॥ ६८७। सिंनाद = सिंहनाद ॥

भिक्षा निले वान्दी साजान करिया ॥ ६९३
भिक्षा नेओ अथीत गोंसाइ ।
गिरिर घरर वान्दी फिरिया घरत याइ ॥ ६९४
दक्षिन भागीया अथीत हामि नाम ब्रह्मचारि ।
वान्दी छाड़र हातत भिक्षा नइते ना पारि ॥ ६९५
यदि भिक्षा देय तवे साइवानि सकल ।
तवे भिक्षा नइते पारि अथीतर कुमर ॥ ६९६
थाक २ अथीत केंकुड़ा वठिया ।
कत क्षन ना पाओ भिक्षा फेउ २ करिया ॥ ६९७
कान्दिया गेल वान्दी कन्यार वरावर ।
दक्षिन भागीया अथीत हामरा नाम ब्रह्मचारि ।
वान्दीर हातर भिक्षा हामरा लइते ना पारि ॥ ६९८
यदि भिक्षा देन तोमार साइवानी सकल ।
येन मते कन्या दुइटा सम्वाद सुनिल ।
भिक्षा धरि कन्या दुइटा खाड़ा हइया रहिल ॥ ६९९
विन छोड़ानि धर्म्मर कपाट आपने खसिल ।
भिक्षा धरि अदुना पदुना वाहिर हइया आइल ॥ ७००
भिक्षा नेओ भिक्षा नेओ अथीत गोंसाइ ।
गिरिर घरर वउ वेटि फिरिया घरत याइ ॥ ७०१
पुरव भागीया अथीत हामि नाम ब्रह्मचारि ।
स्त्री लोकर भिक्षा हामि लइते ना पारि ॥ ७०२
यदि भिक्षा देय तोमार माथार छतर ।
तवे भिक्षा लइते पारि अथीतर कुमर ॥ ७०३
ठांरेया ठांरेया स्त्री आङ्कुल देखाइल ।
स्त्रीर आङ्कुल देखि तोमार हस्तर उपर ।
तोमरा हन आमार माथार छतर ॥ ७०४
तोरा अथीत हामि अथीत एक गुरुर सिस ॥ ७०५
सन्धा कालत एक वाड़ीत उतरिनु याया ।
ठाकरि कालाइर डाइल दिल वियरि धानर चाइल ॥ ७०६
ताहाके खाइल हाऊतासी हइया ।
भेद वमि हइया से गेल मरिया ॥ ७०७
कांछा पाइला डाङ्क माइछ कांछा गोपाल डाङ्क ।
भागत थाकिया आङ्गटि जोड़ा मोक कल्ये दान ॥ ७०८

कानटि गेल वान्दी आमेया पान खाओ।
हस्तिर दाखका काटिया देखो॥ ७०९
मोर सोयामि निवे चिन करिया।
विदेसी अधीत हइले फेलावे मारिया॥ ७१०
हस्तिर दाखका दिले काटिया।
दुर हइते आइसे हस्ति आइल चड़िया॥ ७११
दुर हइते राजाक परनाम करिल।
सुंड़ दिया धरिया राजाक कान्धत चड़ाइल॥ ७१२
एक घड़ि थाकिले हस्ति धैर्य्य धरिया।
यावत ना आइसे कन्या छलना करिया॥ ७१३
हस्तिर पिटि हइते राजा मृत्तिकाय् नामिल।
हस्त धरि कन्या दुइटा राजाक मन्दीरत लइया गेल।
हासिया खेलिया कन्या चिना पुछा दिल॥ ७१४
केमन गुरु तोक ज्ञान दिल सरीरर भितर।
केमन करि याओ तोर मायर वरावर॥ ७१५
सोनाली भोमरा हइल काया वदलिया।
मयनार महले गेल चलिया॥ ७१६
मयनारं वाङ्लाय् याया ऊङ्कार काड़िल।
मयना मति चोरखा सुग्ने उड़ाइया दिल॥ ७१७
एत मयना अज वड़ नाटक।
चटकिया धरिल चड़कार छतर॥ ७१८
आय् २ वाछा मोर दुखिनीर दुलालीया॥ ७१९
माथार केस राजार दुइ अर्द्ध करिया।
जननीर चरने राजा पैल भजिया॥ ७२०
मधु नापितक आनिल डाकिया।
राजा किरा सुद करिवार लागिल।
वामने आसिया नैवद भाना दिल॥ ७२१
संकीर्त्तन राजा करिवार लागिल।
सात गोला धान खयरात करिल॥ ७२२
गभीर नेकुल धरिया वैतरनि हइल पार।
राजार पिता माता वैकुन्ठे हइल पार॥ ७२३
पञ्च लोटा जले मयना छिनान करिया।
हासियाली घरत सोन्दाइल लहर दिया॥ ७२४

७२४। लहर cf. v. 436.॥

एक भात पञ्चास व्यञ्जन रन्धन करिया।
तिन खान लइल अम्बले माजिया॥ ৩২৫
छाड़िर लागिया मयना ऊङ्गार छाड़िल।
तखनि छाड़ी आसिया खाड़ा हइल॥ ৩২৬
प्रथम थाल अन्न दिल छाड़ीर वरावर।
फिर थाल अन्न निले मयना सुन्दर।
फिर थाल अन्न दिले राजार वरावर॥ ৩২৭
हात मुखत जल दिया कोन काम करिल।
श्री कृष्ण वलिया अन्न मुखत तुलि दिल।
एक गास दुइ गास पञ्च गास खाइल॥ ৩২৮
अन्न जल खाइया तुष्ट हइल मन।
भिङ्गार भाड़ीर जले करिल आचमन॥ ৩২৯
कांञो ठेङ्ग तुलिया राजार मस्तके दिल।
कैलासर छाड़ी कैलासत चलि गेल॥ ৩৩০
राजार पाट लइल पुस्कार करिया।
हनुमान दण्ड छत्र वेड़ाइम साजिया।
पाट हस्ति आइल साजिया॥ ৩৩১
राजा कि पोसाक पड़िवार लागिल।
सुड़ दिया धरिया राजाक कान्धत चड़ाइल॥ ৩৩২
वाइज वाजनाय् पाटत लइया गेल।
राजार पाटत परनाम करिल।
सुर दिया धरि राजाक पाटत वसाइल॥ ৩৩৩
देड़ वुड़ि कड़ि खाजना साधिवार लागिल।
राजार राज्यत सुखमय् हइल॥ ৩৩৪

इति॥

I am sorry to say that the above text was copied out by an energetic *bábu* who had the greatest contempt for the dialect it illustrates. He showed his contempt by carefully *correcting* the text, wherever it differed much from his idea of the *sádhu bháshá*. I did not discover this until the first two hundred and fifty verses had been printed off; so, thus far, the above must be taken *cum grano salis*. The principal improvements will be noted in the terminations of the genitive and locative. I may point out here, that Rangpurí possesses an instrumental ending in ए, which may easily be confused with the Bangálí locative. Thus हाते in Rangpurí means "with a hand", while in Bangálí it means "in a hand," of which the Rangpurí would be हातत.

Translation of the Song of Ma'nik Chandra.

1. Think on the name of Ráma, meditate on him with a single mind. If thou utterest the name of Ráma what can Yama do. 2. The wicked man did not utter the name of Ráma in the sloth of his tongue: and even though it was a receptacle of ambrosia, his body was devoured by poison. 3. Who walketh uttering the name of Ráma, along with him goeth a servant of Ráma armed with bow and arrow. 4. The ship that is called by the name of Ráma, hath for its pilot the Holy Master himself. Opening out his arms he crieth out "Come, I will ferry thee across." 5. I have placed the worship of Ráma upon my head. I pause awhile from considering his virtues, and sing the virtues of one who hath accomplished (his path of holiness). By praising him I obtain the accomplishment of my desires.

6. Mánik Chandra was a very pious king in Banga. Each month he used to collect a tax on each plough of seven and a half *gaṇḍas** of *káoṛís*. 7. The people paid a tax of seven and a half *gaṇḍas* of *káoṛís*, and on the day of the *Ashṭamí pújá* used to bring him a herd of goats. 8. The fuel-seller, who supplied him with fuel, had six months' taxes remitted to him in consideration thereof. 9. The leaf-seller, who supplied him with bundles of leaves, had six months' taxes remitted to him in that consideration. 10. Such a king was Mánik Chandra that his *ra'iyats'* fences were built simply of thin reeds; the man who lived at hap-hazard, even he had a horse at his door. So proud were they, that not even the maid-servants wore *sárís* made of jute. 11. No one had need to use the foot-path of another, and no one had to drink the water of another's tank.†

12. From the south there came a *Bangálá* with a long beard; and that *Bangálá*, when he came, made money from the country. 13. Where the tax had formerly been 7½ *gaṇḍas* he took 15 *gaṇḍas*. 14. They sold their ploughs, they sold their yokes, and some sold their ploughshares; through the distress caused by the taxation, some even sold their children at the breast. 15. The misery of the poor unhappy widows became very lamentable; all through the country the villages became broken up. 16. The little *ra'iyats* said to the big *ra'iyats* "Brothers, let us all go to the *pradháns*."‡ 17. Saying, "What advice will all the *pradháns* give," all the *ra'iyats* after consulting together, went to the house of the *pradháns*. 18. "What advice shall we adopt, brothers, and what course of conduct? The king within the kingdom hath become unjust." 19. The *Pradháns* said to all the *ra'iyats*, "This advice I have no power to give; come to S'iva. Let us see what command the mighty Bholánátha will give us." 20. All

* A *buḍi* is five *gaṇḍas* or twenty.

† *i. e.*, every one had his own private path to the *háṭ*, and his own private tank.

‡ The *Rangpurí* term for the village head-man.

the *ra'iyats* after consulting together, went to S'iva's (temple). 21. Calling him "S'iva Ṭhákur," they cried with a loud voice. S'iva Ṭhákur was in the temple, and put his foot outside the door.* 22. When they saw S'iva, all the *ra'iyats* made obeisance. Tying their clothes round their necks, did they make obeisance.

S'IVA SPAKE.

23. "Long may ye live, long may ye live, O *ra'iyats*, may Dharma bless you. May the days of your life be as many as the sands of the sea. 24. Why, why O *ra'iyats*, have ye all come?"

THE RA'IYATS SPAKE.

25. "What advice shall we adopt, and what course of conduct. The king within the kingdom hath become unjust." 26. The ancient S'iva meditated, and after meditating looked up, and found in the fate of the king that the limit of his life was six months distant.

S'IVA SPAKE.

27. "If ye tell this word unto Mayaná she will assuredly destroy my kingdom of Kailáśa."

THE RA'IYATS SPAKE.

28. "One oath, two oaths, three oaths in the name of Hari. If we speak thy word, may we die in great sin." 29. All the *ra'iyats*, after consulting together, went to Śríkalá háṭ. 30. They filled an earthen pot with incense and vermilion. They filled a coop with geese and doves. 31. They also took a white goat, tying him with a rope. Fasting on a Sunday, they took them to a *tírtha* on the Gangá.† 32. They tied the goat at a place sacred to Dharma on the banks of the Gangá, and sacrificed it there.‡ 33. They offered several geese at the *gháṭ*, and burnt incense and vermilion there. 34. They rooted up unblown *binná* grass and brought it. And then wringing out his *languṭi*, he (S'iva) gave vent to the curse; and that curse they (the *ra'iyats*) took up in the corner of their garments.

35. On the Sunday S'iva gave the people this curse. On the Monday the fever seized the king. 36. On the Tuesday the king became weak; on

* It is worth noting how entirely the ideas of the author of the poem are circumscribed by the incidents of his village life. Every one, God or man, acts and lives as if he were a simple *Rangpurí* villager. This verse is an instance. When one *ra'iyat* goes out to see another, it is the village etiquette, to bawl out to him, "*He!* so-and-so," while the visitor is yet a hundred yards or so from the house of him on whom he is about to call. If the latter is "at home," he goes outside his door, and greets the comer. This latter action is called "putting one's foot outside the door." Compare the English expression of "calling on a person."

† By the Gangá, is meant the Brahmaputra. See note to v. 159.

‡ Lit. Dug a hole for the sacrificial post in the same.

the Wednesday he ceased to eat or drink. 37. On the Thursday the king gave up the ghost*: and on the following Tuesday, Chitra Govinda, the accountant of Yama, opened out his account papers. 38. He found in the account papers, that Mánik Chandra had six months to live; and turning his head, he began to speak to Saman Rájá Yama.

YAMA SPAKE.

39. "A king within his kingdom hath become unjust. Bring hither that king within the house of Yama." 40. He began to call for Ábál Yama. He sent a letter (for the king) by Godá Yama.

YAMA SPAKE.

41. "I tell thee Godá Yama, and take thou heed unto my words. Bring Mánik Chandra Rájá here, with his hands and neck tied." 42. He took his leathern rope and his iron hammer, and tied them in a knot; and then Godá Yama started on his journey. 43. Many miles he went, many roads he met. He went a great distance and reached the house of Mánik Chandra. 44. During the six months' illness within the palace, the fair Mayaná did not enquire about the true state of affairs.

THE KING SPAKE.

45. "O Nengá my servant, I tell thee, carry my message: go to Mayaná and tell her about this. 46. Say, 'For six months the king hath been ill within his palace. The King of Kings wisheth to see thee.'" 47. Nengá heard these words and did not tarry. He went off to the palace of Mayaná. 48. Inside the door the Lady Mayaná was playing dice, and through the lattice of the door Nengá made obeisance to her.

MAYANÁ SPAKE.

49. "Why, why, O Nengá hast thou come?"

NENGÁ SPAKE.

50. "Hear, O lady, hear the news; for six months the king hath been ill within his palace. The King of Kings wisheth to see thee." 51. The lady Mayaná became absorbed in contemplation, and, in her contemplation, her eyes fell upon Yama. 52. She took a *bangálá* betel-nut and sweet *miṭha bharí pán* leaf, and divided the nut into two pieces with a knife. 53. In the *pán* leaves she put a little lime, and folded together the *heṭ khili* and the *upar khili.*† 54. She put sixteen scores of charms on the top of

* *Or perhaps* "lost his power of sensation."

† The little conical shaped parcels of prepared *pán*, which we see in the *bazárs*, enclosing a piece of betel-nut and some lime, are called *khilis*. The outside wrapping is made up of two leaves, of which the lower one is called the *heṭ khili*, and the upper one, the *upar khili*.

it; and put the plate of *pán* on the head of the maid-servant. 55. The Lady Mayaná went out, seeing that it was a lucky time, and arrived at the palace of the king.

MAYANÁ SPAKE.

56. "Why and wherefore did the great king summon me?"

THE KING SPAKE.

57. "The king hath been ill for six months in his palace, and the fair Mayaná did not enquire about him."

MAYANÁ SPAKE.

58. "Hear, O king of kings. Learn the magical arts which I have acquired, and then the river of my life will dry up upon thy shoulder.*
59. In my life time great trees will live and die, and we two shall live together in everlasting youth."

THE KING SPAKE.

60. "Hear, O Mayaná: let Yama carry off me, Mánik Chandra; but nevertheless let not the knowledge of a woman be heard by me."† 61.
The king, although offered the arts of women, neglected them; and at exactly midday Cuckold‡ Yama started. 62. He brought the thirsts of death and struck him with them. The king arose crying "Water, water.
63. Give me, O give me water, O fair Mayaná. Give me one vessel of water, and save my life."

MAYANÁ SPAKE.

64. "There are a hundred queens in thy palace. Drink water at their hands, O king of kings."

THE KING SPAKE.

65. "Water, at the hands of even a hundred queens, would smell of fish. It is when I drink at thy hand, that I find great solace."

MAYANÁ SPAKE.

66. "If I go now to bring thee water, that cuckold Yama will bind thee and carry thee away."

* *i. e.* thou wilt live as long as I.

† Lit. my womb.

‡ The word *Bháḍuyá* is an abusive term, and means, more correctly, a man who makes money by the sale of his wife's person.

THE KING SPAKE.

67. "List O Mayaná. Take heed to my words. Place the knife for sacrificing goats upon my bed. 68. When that cuckold Yama cometh, like a Daitya, or a Dánava, him will I strike and slay with the sacrificial knife." 69. As soon as the Lady Mayaná took the vessel in her hands, many men were heard to sneeze,* and many death-watches sounded. 70. Just as the Lady Mayaná passed outside the house, seven men from the seven quarters came in with a noise like thunder. 71. They tied him with leathern thongs, and with an iron mallet they began to beat him.

THE KING SPAKE.

72. "Who beateth me so often? The Lady Mayaná hath gone to fetch me water. Let me fill my belly with one vessel of water."

THE YAMA SPAKE.

73. "Thy wife hath got a boon from Gorakh Náth. If Mayaná meet us, little good will it bode us. She will kneel upon us, and beat us this very midday." 74. Being unable to bear the beating of Yama, the king gave up the ghost, uttering the name of Mayaná. 75. That ghost took Godá Yama and tied it up in his *languṭi*, and to the seven quarters went off the seven men.

76. But Mayaná went to the banks of the Gangá† and spake "Hear, O Gangá, I make known unto thee my petition. 77. There is a king whose worship thou hast enjoyed for these twelve years; give one vessel of water and save his life. 78. For one vessel of water thou shalt have forty-two vessels; therefore do thou restore to life a pious king."

GANGÁ SPAKE.

79. "For whom thou art taking thy vessel full of water; that pious king hath himself been taken away." 80. On hearing this Mayaná began to weep, and hurled away her vessel worth a *lákh* of rupees. 81. Mayaná dived fourteen fathoms beneath the water, and sat in contemplation, and saw that the vermilion on her forehead had become discoloured. 82. She saw that her shell bracelets had turned black, and she broke on her head the two bracelets worth a *lákh* of rupees.

THE BURDEN OF HER SONG.

83. "I have lost my Lord. How many days must I wait and watch for him."

84. Mayaná walked to the palace. When the Lady Mayaná entered the temple, she lit both the front and the rear lamps. 85. Mayaná walked

* Sneezing is a sound of ill omen.

† See note to v. 159.

to Yama's abode; the Lady Mayaná arrived on the banks of the dread river. 86. When Mayaná saw the river she became fearful. It is a river six months wide. The ferry-boat finishes its voyage in a year. Each wave seems vast as mountain peak.

The Burden of her song.

87. "My fate hath become a lot of misery, as Kṛishṇa was of Bindá. The boat is broken and the ropes are worn; how can I pass over, O my guru. That is, if my guru is by me to help me. 88. I will hold the rudder of virtue. O my guru, the boat is broken, and the ropes are worn, but I will cross over."

89. Half her scarf she spread upon the water, and thinking upon virtue, she took her magic seat. 90. Mayaná uttered the words "*tuḍu, tuḍu,*" and the journey of six months was accomplished in six quarters of an hour. 91. She walked to Yama's palace, where thirty-six *krors* of Yamas were sitting in the hall of audience. 92. As soon as the Lady Mayaná stood in Yama's abode, on this side and on that side the Yamas began to run away. 93. When Mayaná came to Yama's palace, she spread great alarm; some got colic and some got pains in their heads. 94. She became a Muhammadan doctor and a Hindu doctor, and extracted the poison from their bodies; but when she came to give them medicine every one ran away. 95. As soon as Godá Yama cast eyes on Mayaná, he ran away as fast as his legs would carry him to his own palace. 96. He went to his own palace and hid himself in a room, and from where she, the Lady Mayaná, was, she lost sight of him. 97. The Lady Mayaná went into contemplation and gazed about, and in her contemplation she saw him in his room. 98. Mayaná collected herself together, and laid aside her own proper form. She put on the appearance of a gardener's wife, and went into the palace of Godá Yama. 99. "Godá, Godá", Mayaná cried to him with a loud voice. 100. As soon as Godá Yama saw Mayaná he burst through the *ṭáṭí* walls of his palace and ran away*. 101. Mayaná cried "*már már*" and chased him through a treeless field, where a hundred ploughmen were ploughing. Like a deer did Mayaná chase Yama. 102. Thence Godá Yama lost his senses and turned himself into a prawn, and jumped into the sea. 103. The Lady Mayaná went into contemplation and gazed about, and in her contemplation her eyes fell on the prawn. 104. Mayaná uttered "*tuṛu tuṛu*" with a terrible cry, and changed herself into forty-two buffalos, who jumped into the sea. 105. Eating cress she chased Yama. In mid-sea she caught Yama by the neck. 106.

* Compare note on v. 21. All the houses of the peasantry in Rangpur are built of *ṭáṭí* (mat) walls. When a thief is caught in such a house, he attempts, usually successfully, to escape by bursting through these flimsy obstructions.

There Godá Yama, mighty as the thunder-bolt, burst the staff she held in her right hand and fled. 107. Thence Godá Yama lost his senses and he became a minnow and began to swim in the water. 108. Leaving her former shape, Mayaná concentrated herself and became a *Pánkáuṛi* and *Vánoyár*,* by a change of her form. 109. With flappings of her wings she chased him, and in mid-sea she snapped up Godá Yama in her bill. 110. Then Godá Yama, mighty as the thunder-bolt, thrust Mayaná off, and ran away. 111. Thereafter what did Godá Yama do? He became an eel, and hid himself in the mud. 112. Thence the Lady Mayaná went into contemplation, and her eyes fell upon him in the mud. 113. Mayaná uttered "*tuḍu, tuḍu*" with a terrible cry, she became a swan; pecking at the mud she chased Godá Yama, and in mid-sea she seized Godá Yama by the neck. 114. He thrust off the Lady Mayaná and fled away. He cast aside his former form, and Godá Yama concentrated himself. 115. He took the form of a maggot and went off to Pátála. 116. When he arrived at Pátála, Yama twisted his beard (boastfully). "Now, how will the *śyálí*, the Lady Mayaná, recognize me." 117. The Lady Mayaná went into contemplation and gazed about, and in her contemplation her eyes fell on the maggot. 118. Leaving her former shape Mayaná concentrated herself, and became an ant by a change of her form. 119. She went to the world of Pátála, and, seizing Godá Yama by the throat, gradually pulled him up out of the ground. 120. Leaving her former shape Mayaná concentrated herself, and became her ownself by a change of form. 121. She threw him down on his face, and began to belabour Godá Yama. She continued belabouring him till her hands were weary. She then turned him on his back, and began to kick him. 122. Then Godá Yama, mighty as the thunder-bolt, became a house pigeon and flew off to the sky. 123. Mayaná changed her shape, and became a falcon and a hawk, and she pecked at him and cast Godá Yama down from heaven. 124. Thence Godá Yama lost his senses, and became a mouse changing his form. 125. He went to Kaṭhiyá the oilman's house, and hid himself under his *máchá*.† 126. The Lady Mayaná went into contemplation and gazed about, and in her contemplation her eyes fell upon the mouse. 127. Leaving her former shape Mayaná concentrated herself, and became a cat by a change of form. 128. She changed herself from being one cat into forty-two cats, and surrounded the house of Kaṭhiyá the oilman. 129. One *daṇḍa*, two *daṇḍas*, three *daṇḍas* passed, and the ill-natured woman caught good-natured Godá Yamá. 130. She made him descend from the *máchá*, and with a sudden leap the Lady Mayaná seized him by the neck. 131. Thence Godá Yama, mighty as the thunder-bolt, slipped out between the interstices of her claws and fled.

* Two kinds of fish-eating birds. † A bamboo bench.

132. Yama left his former shape, and concentrated himself. He became a *Vaishṇava* and changed his form. 133. He used the earth castings of crabs instead of sandal-wood paste, and made his rosary of *Sáil* seeds. 134. Hopefully he took a branch of a castor-oil tree (for his stick), and going into a *Vaishṇava pújá* house, sat himself amongst the worshippers. 135. The Lady Mayaná went into contemplation and gazed about, and in her contemplation her eyes fell upon the *Vaishṇava*. 136. Mayaná gave up her former shape. She concentrated herself, and took that of a bee. 137. In the place of one bee she became forty-two bees, and set out for the place of worship, and she flew around the heads of all the *Vaishṇavas* there. 138. All the *Vaishṇavas* said, "Brothers, hear the news. What sinful *Vaishṇava* is in this assembly?" 139. As soon as Godá Yama saw the bees, he slipped under the quilts of the *Vaishṇavas*. 140. As soon as the Lady Mayaná found out where he was, she settled down upon Yama's neck. 141. Not being able to bear the stings of the bees, Godá Yama ran away from the place. 142. Mayaná laid aside her bee-shape, and, after concentrating herself, took her own form. 143. She seized Godá Yama, and plucked up from the ground an armful of *eluyá* grass. 144. Fifty-two times sixteen scores of ropes she twisted, sitting at a place where three roads meet,* and tied her own waist to that of Godá Yama. Then she carried off Godá Yama beating him with a rod of cane.

Mayaná spake.

145. "Hear, O Godá Yama, while I make my petition. Set free my husband, who is my only wealth."

Godá Yama spake.

146. "Thy husband I will not set free", and thereupon Mayaná began to weep.

The burden of her song.

147. "My husband is no longer in my house, O lord of the unhappy. For whom shall I abide in the days of my youth?"

148. Mayaná uttered "*tuḍu, tuḍu*" with a terrible cry, and all the Heavenly Munis came down on hearing her voice. 149. In a chariot of flowers, came Gorakh the Vidyádhara. Riding upon a flail, came Nárada

* The fact that a place, where three roads meet, is considered especially favourable for performing magical rites, is worth noticing. I need hardly draw attention to similar customs obtaining in Europe. In Tirhut,—it is customary, when a person is sick, to cast away at midnight at a place where three roads meet, an offering of some yellow cloth, a fowl, and some condiments, over which some charms have been recited. It is believed that the disease will then leave the sick man, and seize upon the wayfarer who first comes across the offering in the morning.

the best of munis. 150. On the back of Vásoyá came Bholá, the lord of the world. Riding on a bow and arrow came Ráma Chandra and Lakshmaṇa. 151. The five Páṇḍava brothers came down here and there; there is no counting the number of munis who came from heaven. 152. Mayaná parted her hair in two, and fell at the feet of Gorakh Náth.

MAYANÁ SPAKE.

153. "Help, help, O Gorakh the Vidyádhara. He hath carried off my husband, who is all my wealth. He will not give back my husband, who is my wealth."

GORAKH NA'TH SPAKE.

154. "Hear my words. All the munis have taken advice, and have blessed thee, Lady Mayaná. 155. Go, O Mayaná, we give to thee a boon. Let there be a fœtus developed for seven months now within thy womb." 156. Even as the munis blessed her, her body which was as light as *solá* (pith) gradually became heavy.

THE MUNIS SPAKE.

157. "In eighteen months, it will be born, in its nineteenth year it will die. But, if it worship a Háḍi's feet with steadfast mind, it will not die." 158. On hearing this Mayaná delayed there no longer. She started for her palace and arrived there in safety. 159. She took nine *káoṛís* in her hand, and departed to the banks of the Gangá.* 160. With the nine *káoṛís* she bought a piece of land, and then returned to her own palace. 161. She broke up the old house and made a bier, and with it went some firewood on litters on men's shoulders. 162. Oil, *ghí*, mustard, and sesamum began to go. She called all her relations, and she cut some fresh bamboos and made a bier. 163. She took the pious king away upon the bier she had prepared, and the Lady Mayaná herself was carried off upon the door of the house. 164. Mayaná began to sing the Song of the Excellence of Hari. She began to praise him as she was carried to the river's bank. 165. She built a funeral pyre running north and south, she buried posts and made a platform. 166. By the side of each post she set a jar of *ghí*. Beneath each of them she set a jar of oil. Mustard seed and sesamum she scattered over the pyre. 167. Mayaná uttered the words "Guru, Guru" with a terrible cry, and Gorakh Náth came there and stood visible.

MAYANÁ SPAKE.

168. "Protect me, O protect me, O Gorakh the Vidyádhara."

* It must be noted, that throughout this poem, the word Gangá does not refer to the river commonly known as the Ganges. It always refers to the Brahmaputra.

GORAKH NÁTH SPAKE.

"Go forth Mayaná, I have given thee a boon. Within the fire thou shalt perceive the cold of Mágha. 169. Mayaná began to spread vermilion all over her forehead. 170. She put on a silken scarf. She took a golden knife and a mango branch in her hand, and she laid out the king towards the north and south. 171. Mayaná laid the king's head on her right hand, and she put her own head on his left hand. 172. In each household a citizen gave one piece of firewood. The pile of firewood almost touched the sky as well as the earth. 173. Water and sandal-wood did Chandra, the merchant, scatter upon the pyre. Not a single near relation was present to set it alight. 174. One who lived near the door of the king,—a bráhmaṇ *guru*,—stretched forth his hand and applied the torch. 175. Each relation cast one vessel of water on the pyre. Together they lustrated the pyre, once, twice, and five times. Saying "*Hari bol*," they set it alight. 176. E'en as the fire smelt the smell of the *ghí*, it blazed up with a great roar. 177. For seven days and nine nights Mayaná stayed within the blaze, and even her apparel though offered to the flames did not take fire. 178. Mayaná burnt the body of the pious king, and placed the ashes in her lap. There sat Mayaná, like a *Gosvámí* in his house. 179. Mayaná burnt the body of the pious king and the smoke rose up to heaven. There sat the Lady Mayaná like unmelted gold. 180. The little relations said to the big relations, "Brothers, thrust at her. Let all the relations thrust at her." 181. The Lady Mayaná is sitting within the fire. She cries: "Hear, O relations, I have a child of seven months in my womb. Let not all the relations thrust at me." 182. The little relations said to the big relations, "Brothers, let us go to Chánd the merchant, and ask his advice. 183. Ye know Chánd the merchant from childhood. Let us see what answer he will give." 184. Behind the door sat the merchant playing dice; and through the lattice, did they make reverence to him.

CHA'ND SPAKE.

185. "Why, O relations, why and wherefore have ye all come?"

THE RELATIONS SPAKE.

186. "For seven days and nine nights Mayaná hath been in the fire, and yet the Fair Mayaná hath not been burnt."

CHA'ND SPAKE.

187. "This Mayaná hath obtained a boon from Gorakh Náth. Fire doth not burn her, nor doth she sink in water. Were the three worlds to come to an end, she would not go to Yama's abode. And yet, O relations, ye wish to slay her. 188. Sit ye in a place where three roads meet, and

twist of grass fifty-two *krors* of ropes; carry ye off a stone weighing twenty-two *mans*. 189. Thrust her forth from the fire, and tie ye the twenty-two *man* stone upon her chest. 190. Cast ye Mayaná and the ashes of the fire away on the stream, that they may float away. Then bathe ye and return to your homes." 191. On hearing this the relations no longer stayed. They carried away the stone of twenty-two *mans*. 192. They thrust the Lady Mayaná forth from the fire, and tied the stone of twenty-two *mans* on her chest. 193. They cast her and the ashes upon the stream, and bathed and returned to their homes.

194. At the expiration of eighteen months and eighteen days Mayaná became filled, and then the (future) pious king turned himself in her womb. "I die, I die," said Mayaná, and she began to weep. 195. She brought into use her magical art called *kharupá* (the art of cutting), and by it she cut open her fifty-two *krors* of ropes. 196. "I die, I die," said Mayaná, as she landed at the foot of a *Ním* tree; and as she ascended, a sound was heard like unto the roaring of heaven in the intermediate quarters. 197. The Mahárája fell upon the ground amid the after-birth and birth waters; and he began to cry, saying "*omyá* and *chomyá*." 198. The little relations said to the big relations, "Brothers, let us go and see whose child is crying thus." 199. They took one step, and they took two steps, and they arrived at the spot. Mayaná said unto them. "Hear, O relations and mark my words. 200. Decorate the *pálkí* of the old king and bring it here, and take this child-king to the palace." 201. They decorated the *pálkí* of the old king and brought it, and they mounted the pious king within it. 202. Big drums, and little drums, guitars, and cymbals sounded in all directions. Cymbals, side drums and kettle-drums sounded in all directions. 203. There was firing of guns and a thick darkness caused by the smoke. Father could not recognize son; he only could call for him. 204. There was a poor man who had a child in the kingdom, and he could not give it food and water in his own house. 205. So he cast it down at a place where three roads meet, amidst its after-birth and birth waters. 206. That child did Mayaná also take up into her bosom, and carry to the palace.

Mayaná spake.

207. "I say unto thee, my maid-servant, pay attention to my words." 208. The maid-servant went and called the wet-nurse and brought her. 209. The wet-nurse cut the navel strings of both the children. She took all the presents that Mayaná gave, and went to her own house. 210. What with to-day and what with to-morrow seven days passed, and during the seven days the king caused a concert of flutes and drums to be made. 211. What with to-day and what with to-morrow, ten days passed, and after ten days the king held the first *śráddha* after his father's death. 212.

On the thirteenth day the king held the final *śráddha*, and held a concert of drums and cymbals, and all the relations came and sacrificed. 213. He gave a feast to all his relations, and at that hour the Lady Mayaná first touched fish. 214. What with to-day, and what with to-morrow, a year passed, and after one year another day came. 215. What with to-day, and what with to-morrow, five years passed, and she gave him to be taught by a *guru*. 216. He taught the king to write in four lessons. What with to-day, and what with to-morrow, seven years passed. 217. The king was then named. Mánik Chandra Rájá's son was called Gopí Chandra. 218. And his younger (foundling) brother was called Lankeśwar "Found in the Field."* 219. What with to-day, and what with to-morrow, nine years passed; and then, what did the Lady Mayaná do? 220. She spake as follows to the *Guru* bráhmaṇ.

Mayaná spake.

221. "Go, go, O *guru* bráhmaṇ, pay attention to my words. Go quickly before the king Haríś Chandra. 222. He has two daughters in his palace, named Aduná and Paduná. Arrange a marriage between them and my son, and return." 223. The Reverend Bráhmaṇ on hearing these words did not delay. But hastened to the palace of king Harís' Chandra. 224. He cried out with a loud voice "Ho! King Harís' Chandra."† The king was in his house and he stepped out. 225. The reverend and learned Bráhmaṇ made salutation. 226. The king gave him a god-like throne to sit upon, and after supplying him with camphor and betel, enquired as follows. 227. "Why and wherefore, O *guru* bráhmaṇ, hast thou come so great a distance?"

The Bra'hmaṇ spake.

228. "Mayaná hath sent me to thy presence. In thy palace are two damsels named Aduná and Paduná. The fair Mayaná wisheth to form a marriage with them. 229. Mayaná hath a son within her palace, and to him doth she wish to give them."

The King spake.

230. "Go, go, I consent," and ordered him away. And the Bráhmaṇ on hearing this returned to Mayaná. 231. They took a load of betel nuts and a load of *pán* leaves. And five bráhmaṇs began to cut the betel and the *pán*. 232. They cut the betel and *pán* and searched for a

* He is also called Khetu, or Khetuwá, and appears to have become Gopí Chandra's servant. He took over his concubines when the latter went on his pilgrimage. See also note to verse 290.

† Compare note to v. 21.

lucky day, and then did they fix the time of the marriage. 233. On the Saturday, Mayaná fasted, and on the Sunday, she made arrangements for the marriage. 234. They planted five plantain trees in King Harís' Chandra's palace, and they lit the golden lamps and the censers on the day fixed. 235. They then sent for five singing women, and cries of "*ulu, ulu*" were heard around. 236. He gave Aduná in marriage, he gave Paduná, and he gave a hundred maid-servants to wait upon them. 237. He gave as wedding-presents a hundred villages, and a hundred elephants. 238. He gave as wedding presents a hundred horses and a hundred cows. 239. After giving them in marriage he allowed them to depart. And immediately afterwards the Lady Mayaná sent an invitation to all the kings of all the kingdoms. 240. From that time that pious king was called Gopí Chandra.

241. After eighteen years, at the advice of his aged mother he became a *Sanyásí*. 242. A hundred beautiful damsels, weeping, fell at his feet, "O pious king, do not depart and leave us."

THE QUEEN SPAKE.

243. "Nay, nay, thou shalt not go, my King, to a far country. For whom but thee, have I built up this cold dreary house (of my life). 244. I built a humble* dwelling, nor yet is it sullied by old age. Why art thou leaving me in my youth, and turning my bridehood into vanity? 245. In my dreams shall I see my king. I shall throw my arm on the couch; but the wealth of my life will not be there. 246. Behold, every† mother and sister of a man of modest wealth shall have her master to sleep upon her bosom, while I, unhappy one, will remain weeping in an empty house. 247. When a house is empty and the doors are closed, men come and kick the walls outside. In the time of her youth all voices cast scandal at a widow. 248. Therefore shalt thou take me with thee. I am the life, the wealth of thy life; let thy damsel go with thee. 249. In the time of thy hunger I will cook thy food. When thou art thirsty I will give thee to drink. 250. In mirth and laughter will I pass the night. 251. If we have a long field to traverse, I will wile away the time in talk. When we approach the dwelling of a householder, there will I reverence thee like my *guru*. 252. A cool mat‡ will I spread for thee; on a pillow shalt thou rest thy feet. Laughing and joking will I shampoo thy body. 253. When I hurt thy hand I will shampoo thy feet, and amidst our sport and laughter, I will devour thy bosom, and thou shalt devour

* Lit. pent-roofed.

† Lit. ten. This use of "ten" for "every," is of frequent occurrence in Rangpur. Thus *Das' jan ki kay?* is the stock expression equivalent to "What do people say?"

‡ *Vulgo. Seetul-pat.*

mine. 254. In the hot season will I fan thy countenance with a palm leaf. In the cold month of Mágha I will nestle into thy body for warmth, 255. In the cold month of Mágha I will cook for thee spiced viands.* Indra's favourite sweetmeat, the lap of a hundred wives, will I alone cause thee to enjoy."

THE KING SPAKE.

256. "List, O daughter of king Haríś Chandra. In many varied ways art thou displaying thy charms, nor can I bear them. 257. Thy teeth are white as the *solá* pith, from eating the *Vansa Hari* nut. When thou speakest, they glisten (like white flowers), and the bees come humming towards them. 258. If thou goest with me, thou wilt be a woman of fresh and fair appearance, and I will be a man clad in one rough blanket. When they see us, all the people will say—'There goeth a pilgrim, but he is a stealer of women.' 259. And if they say this, no householder will give us shelter. In thy word and in mine, O daughter of a prince, will they put no trust."

THE QUEEN SPAKE.

260. "Hear me, my King, thou loved one not to be deceived.† One petition, and no more I make unto thee. 261. Like thee will I put around my neck a Ráma rosary. Like thee will I wear nought but a single tight and scanty cloth. 262. My two breasts will I tie up in tattered clothes. I will break six of my front teeth. My tresses which hang down unto my knees, them let me cut and cast away. 263. I will take in my hand a hollow gourd. I will cast a rough blanket round my neck. I too will become a pilgrim. Following thy footsteps will I beg for alms."

THE BURDEN OF HER SONG.‡

264. "O! the pipe of S'yám. My mind whirls. My eyes flow with tears."

THE KING SPAKE.

265. "O mighty fate. I am encompassed amidst a net of charms. What love is this which I have for a woman. 266. If thou goest with me, thou wilt be going with a pilgrim. There there are tigers of the wood, and when thou seest them thou wilt be afraid. There there are tigers of the wood, and great is the fear of them that be mighty. 267. When a

* Lit. curries made of cold weather chillies.

† Lit. "English."

‡ This *Duyá* forms the first verse of a song in honour of Kṛishṇa, which is given in the appendix.

man and a woman, in such plight as thou and I, go along the road; the tiger of the wood seizeth the woman and eateth her. 268. Whether the tiger eat thee or eat thee not, he will assuredly kill thee. Why therefore wilt thou kill thyself because thou wouldest follow an ascetic."

269. The damsel began to laugh freely.

THE QUEEN SPAKE.

"Who sayeth these words? and who believeth them? 270. What tiger slayeth and eateth the woman that goeth with her husband? These words are but to deceive, and a pretext for thy flight. 271. Let the tiger of the wood devour me, I fear him not. It is better to die at the feet of my husband than to lead a life of perpetual disgrace. 272. Thou wilt be my banyan tree, and I will be thy creeper. To thy feet will I cling, and then whither wilt thou flee? 273. When I was in my father's house, O pious king, why didst thou not then become a pilgrim? 274. Now I have become a comely woman, and worthy of thee. If thou leavest me and becomest an ascetic, I will surely die. 275. Let the stream of my youth fall down before thee. When the hairs of my head turn gray, then do thou turn pilgrim. 276. The branches of fair jasmines bend down to the ground (with age). I am now a full grown woman, and how long shall I retain my comeliness? 277. How long shall I keep my youth, e'en though I bind it and tie it down. For continually my heart weepeth for my husband."

THE BURDEN OF HER SONG.

278. "Thou hast wedded me, and thou art going. I weep for thee. Thou hast thy father, and thy brethren; but I, unhappy one, have none. I have left them all for thee, O king."

279. He had chosen Aduná and Paduná, and had married them. A *bhaṭṭa* bráhmaṇ had named her Aduná. 280. He himself had called her Aduná and given her maid-servants.

THE KING SPAKE.

"How can I break such love in my house? 281. I will take alms from one door, and will go to the door of another: easily will I lose my Kshetri birth and my Baniyá caste. 282. Where'er I shall see a woman like thee, my youthful lovely wife, there weeping will I lay me down and die. 283. Where'er I shall see a woman like my lovely wife. First will I address her as 'mother,' and then will I ask for alms."

THE QUEEN SPAKE.

284. "Alas, alas, my own husband, thou hast uttered a black word. Thou hast married me in my childhood, and thou desertest me in my youth."

THE KING SPAKE.

285. "Now also wait thou with thy hand upon thy heart. Until I return after fifty years have passed away."

THE QUEEN SPAKE.

285. "Lift up thy head, O king, and see a pair of juicy cocoa-nuts over my heart. The pair of cocoa-nuts shine forth with lustre. 287. I will open the nuts and put them to thy mouth, thou hast not strength in thy body (to pluck them). It is a fruit, which if a man refuse, he will suffer the pangs of hell four times fourteen times.

THE KING SPAKE.

288. "Hear me, O lady, daughter of Hariś Chandra. When a secret hath been divulged, the meaning of its words become plain. 289. In front rideth an elephant's *mahául*, behind him the king. Far have I gone, and (I have learned that) the great house of my pilgrimage is at a far distance. 290. I have tasted the fruit of the cocoanut and my belly was not filled. In vain have I, a householder, suffered* in my servitude."

THE QUEEN SPAKE.

291. "Hear me, my king. My pleasant loved one, one petition have I to make unto thee. 292. "Do not, O pious king, go to a far country. Give me one little child, that I may keep him in my lap. 293. I will keep him and nurse him in my lap, and I will touch thee when I see my darling child. 294. I will place the sun-shade and staff of thy royalty over my child's head. I will be the mother of the king and will enjoy the kingdom." 295. The queen spoke of a child, and the king heard her words and said,

THE KING SPAKE.

296. "What thou desirest is not a *chíní chámpá* plantain, that I may mix it with water and give it thee to eat. It is not the fruit of a tree, that I can pluck it, and place it in thy hands. 297. Fate hath not given thee a child. What can I do? 298. I will repeat the charms of the *gurus* of old, and will become a seven months' child within thy womb. 299. Thou shalt call me 'son.' Thou shalt open the covering of thy breast, and shalt give me milk."

THE QUEEN SPAKE.

300. "I spake to thee of a child, and thou speakest to me of milk. Thou art my wedded husband, how can I call thee 'son.' 301. I knew

* Lit. Died. A popular song makes Gopí Chandra charge his wives with intriguing with Khetuwá Lankes'var as a last resource for getting away. But this is not borne out by any copy of this poem which I have seen.

not, O king, that there were but a sheep* and a jackal within thy heart. Not one *káoṛí* of sense hast thou in thy body. 302. (Thy mother) because she is a widow, wisheth to make her daughter-in-law a widow too. Even if my husband pass her house, (jealously) doth she turn her eyes upon him."

THE KING SPAKE.

303. "Ha! thou daughter of a vile one; thou hast abused my mother. I might have stayed a few days, but I will go to-morrow." 304. He could not bear the childishness of the damsel, and so the fair king went to the place of audience. 305. (There was a grove) of twelve *supárí* trees and thirteen *tál* trees, and in its shade sat the king's son. 306. The bráhmaṇs and the relations all sat in a row, and Bír Si*m*h, his Bháṇḍárí, gave him the accounts of the kingdom. 307. On a golden seat sat Mayaná with her feet on a silver stool. The Lady Mayaná went to the audience of her good son. 308. The full cutcherry hummed with the noise of the crowd, and there the fair Mayaná stood. 309. When the king saw his mother, he made obeisance; as he made obeisance, he tied his cloth around his neck.

MAYANA' SPAKE.

310. "Long live the widow's son. May Dharma bless him. May the years of his life be many as the sands of the sea. 311. I thought the widow's son had gone to be a pilgrim; but lo, till to-day he is here with his fair wife. 312. The Satya Yuga is passed, we are in the second Yuga, the third Yuga will come. But in the Kali Yuga sons will marry early. 313. The Kali era is a foul era, and hath now approached. Each sitteth alone and enjoyeth another's wealth. 314. Kings will no longer do justice in their kingdom, and sons will no longer offer sacrifices for their fathers. 315. Wives will no longer be faithful to their husbands. Pupils will no longer reverence their teachers. 316. Behold, four miscreants went to destruction. 317. The miscreant who doth not reverence his teacher, him even jackals will not eat. Even crows will not touch the body of a Vaishṇava. 318. Let a miscreant be cast into fire and he becometh dust and ashes. Let him float upon the water and he becometh food for fishes. 319. He is buried beneath the earth and he becometh food for worms. No where do I see salvation for a miscreant."

THE BURDEN OF HER SONG.

320. "My darling blue lotus, how canst thou become an eremite? Men will say there goeth one who hath no mother." 321. The king made up his mind to be a pilgrim, and at a cross-road his queen began to weep.

* *I. e.* That your heart contained nothing but cowardice and treachery.

THE QUEEN SPAKE.

322. "How canst thou wish to go to a far country? Oh wait and pass the charms of Mayaná through an ordeal. 323. Oh put her to the test of burning oil. If she survive that ordeal, then shave thy head and go forth a pilgrim." 324. The king heard this and hastened to the hall of audience. 325. He sat in the audience chamber, and could not make up his mind. Often and often he called for his servant Khetu, his younger brother.

THE KING SPAKE.

326. "My servant Khetu, take heed unto my words. Go* unto my mother's palace." 327. On hearing this, the servant did not delay. 328. "Say this to Mayaná—('Thy son) would put thee to the test (of burning oil')." 329. Hearing these words, Mayaná laughed. "This is not thy thought, but a conspiracy between thy wives. All the thoughts they teach thee, will become barren. 330. Instead of one ordeal, I will pass through seven, and then will the Prince leave his house."

THE KING SPAKE.

331. "I say unto thee, Khetu, and take thou heed unto my words. 332. Build thou up a furnace deep and wide. Strip off the three fibres of three cocoa-nuts, and place the bare (nuts round the furnace as supports for the cauldron)." 333. Khetu set a cauldron holding sixty *mans* upon the furnace, and into the cauldron he poured eighty† *mans* of oil. 334. He cast upon the flames fuel of *sál* wood, and set it blazing. Over all he placed a cover. 335. For seven days he ceaselessly added fuel. 336. One day, two days, five days passed. After seven days he lifted the cover. 337. "The oil is hot, even as fire," such words did Khetu speak unto the king. 338. "Thy servant was ordered to make (preparations for) the ordeal by oil. 339. What command hath the king of kings for his servant?"

THE KING SPAKE.

"Go and say this unto my mother. 340. 'The ordeal by oil is ready before the king. The king doth summon thee; O Mother, come quickly'."

MAYANA' SPAKE.

341. "Do I eat at thy fathers' hand, or at the hands of the fathers of the king. At thy command, what ordeal shall I pass through?" 342.

* Note the force of चलु here, and in vv. 328 and 332. It has entirely lost any special meaning of its own; and is used as a pure expletive to add strength to an imperative.

† Sic in original.

These words Khetu told the king, who heard them, and became furiously enraged. 343. The king took his evening towel for washing his body, and flung it to Khetu. 344. And Khetu shook that towel, and with it bound tightly the lady Mayaná, and cast her into the oil. 345. Even as the lady Mayaná fell amid the oil, the flames rushed up with a roar to heaven. 346. Mayaná sunk into the oil up to her neck, and, as she did so, she took the oil into her hands and patted it into her head as if she were bathing. 347. Seeing calamity (approaching) the king became furiously enraged. He called Khetu, calling him, "Slave, slave," and began to abuse him. 348. "Lift up the cover and place it over my mother, and for nine days continuously, do thou add fuel to the flames." 349. One day, two days, three days passed away. But Mayaná concentrated herself and took the form of a grain of mustard. 350. After nine days, Khetu lifted up the cover and when he could not see the queen, he began to cry. 351. Thus did he say unto the king. "Thy mother is dead, and gone to Yama's abode. 352. Wherefore dost thou keep thy *págaṛí* on thy head? Behold (I am unclean) and the assembly of bráhmaṇs will not drink water at my hand." 353. The king cried "Mother, mother" and began to weep.

THE BURDEN OF HIS SONG.

354. "Fate hath made me motherless, O lord of the unhappy. Such was written in my destiny. No longer will I see my mother." 355. He took a handful of twigs in his hand and began to search amidst the oil. 356. Once, twice and thrice he searched. At the third time of searching he fished up the towel. No trace of Mayaná's body was within the fire. 357. Sixteen men took the cauldron on their shoulders, and they flung out the oil at a place where three roads meet. 358. With a loud roar the flames rose to heaven, but Mayaná in her form of a mustard seed remained hidden in the *Dub* grass. 359. Suddenly Khetu began to weep, and when she heard the sound of his weeping, Mayaná felt pity for him.

MAYANA' SPAKE.

360. "Weep not, weep not, Khetu, my servant. Cease thy tears. I am Mayaná. I have not been burnt within the furnace." 361. He took up the sixty-*man* cauldron in his hand and brought it before the king. 362. Mayaná in fact underwent seven ordeals, and passed them all.

THE KING SPAKE.

363. "Hear, O lady Mayaná, my mother. From what *siddha* hast thou learnt thy magic arts?"

MAYANA' SPAKE.

364. "Thou askest me from what holy man I have learned my arts. I have learned them from Gorakh Náth himself. 365. I tell thee, learn

thou thy knowledge from Kholá the Háḍi." 366. When the king heard the name of a Háḍi, he stopped his ears with his hands. For she had uttered an impious word with her tongue.

THE KING SPAKE.

367. "A Háḍi is of a vile caste. He cleanseth privies and doth not bathe. Shall I, a king, make obeisance to a Háḍi for twenty-two *daṇḍas!*

MAYANÁ SPAKE.

368. "Hear me, my child, speak thy words in a whisper, so that the Háḍi may not hear. If he cursed thee, thou wouldest die at once. 369. Thy subjects feed their lamps with oil and ghí: but that Háḍi feedeth his lamp with merely Gangá water. 370. As many lamps as there are in the houses of thy subjects, so many hath that Háḍi in his little hut. 371. In whosesoever house he eateth, to whosesoever house he goeth, simply at the word of his mouth he causeth the sea to stop its motion." 372. The king sat in his audience chamber and could not make up his mind. Repeatedly he called his servant Khetu, his younger brother. 373. "Where hast thou gone, my brother? First would I eat *pán*,* then I would have the *paṇḍit* of the days of my father come to me." 374. Khetu heard these words and made no delay. He hastened towards the *paṇḍit's* house. 375. "I say unto thee, O reverend *paṇḍit*, and pay thou heed unto my words. The king would see thee in his palace. Haste thee to the hall of audience." 376. He dressed himself in a *dhuṭi* of modest kind. Loosening out his brahmanical cord, so that the threads appeared in pairs, he passed it round his neck. 377. He took his papers relating to the Almanac under his arm, and proceeded to the king's hall of audience. 378. The hall was full, the crowd gave forth a confused noise. At this time did the *paṇḍit*, the son of a *paṇḍit*, present himself. 379. "Incarnation of justice" he said and made obeisance. "Tutelary Deity of my family" said the king making obeisance in return. 380. He called him "Reverend Brother," and made him sit upon the couch. "O reverend Sir, thou art the crest-jewel among prophets. 381. What day will the king sew for himself a beggar's wallet and quilt? What day will the king shave his head? 382. What day will the great king besmear himself with ashes? What day will the pious king pierce his two ears? 383. What day will the pious king wear nought but a *languṭi?* What day will I carry a beggar's platter in my hand? 384. What day will I start for a far country? Read me aright, and prophesy me this." 385. Taking every precaution to ensure good luck, he produced his Almanac. Such power was there in that Almanac that it could speak itself.

* That is to say, "immediately." Chewing *pán* is such a mechanical and continuous action with a Rangpurí man or woman, that the phrase "to do a thing after eating *pán*", means to do it at once. Cf. vv. 398, 553 and 692.

The Book spake.

386. "On Tuesday will he sew his wallet and his quilt. On Wednesday will he shave his head. 387. On Thursday will he besmear himself with ashes. On Friday the king shall pierce his two ears. 388. On Friday the king shall pierce his ears, and on Saturday shall he put on a *languṭi.* 389. On Sunday the king shall take in his hand a beggar's platter; on that day the king shall set out for a far country. 390. He will take thee from thy home and will give thee advice and hope. For some days he will distress thee in the midst of the forest. Other sorrow will he give thee in the sandy waste. 391. Other sorrow will he give thee in the city of S'ríkalá. He will pawn thee for food in the house of Hírá the Harlot. 392. The Harlot's dress will be a linen *sárí* bright as fire. Thy dress, O king, will be a knotted rope. 393. Unsifted rice will she give thee and *brinjals* full of seeds. She will give thee *brinjals* full of seed, and thou wilt burn them and eat them. A pitiless harlot is she; thou wilt be forbidden oil and salt. 394. The harlot will seek the privy, and it wilt be thou who wilt cleanse it. Thou shalt close thy eyes, and proffer her the water of her sin.* 395. Early in the morning shalt thou rise, and she will beat thee with a broom. Thou shalt lift up the bed of her sins, of countless, countless sins. 396. *Bhángí* ropes will she give thee and a *bhángí* stick and two water jars. Twelve loads shalt thou measure out every day."

The King spake.

397. "Hear, Reverend Sir. Happiness and misery are written in our destiny. Methinks, I see death written by the Creator in my fate. 'Tis not in two syllables and a half that it can be cancelled." 398. Brother Khetu, where art thou gone? First would I eat *pán.* Then would I give the Bráhmaṇ a present and bid him good speed." 399. He gave him a present and bade him speed. "Make present the barber of my father's time." 400. He went to the *nápit* and called him to the king, saying "Brother, fetch thy razors and come." 401. The hall was full. The crowd gave forth a confused noise. At this time did the barber, the son of a barber, present himself. 402. Even as the pious king saw the barber, he descended from his throne†; and as he did, the theatrum of the temple, and other walled buildings fell to the ground. 403. The forest trees, and the shrubs, the very leaves of the trees began to weep. The forest deer bent their heads

* Not a literal translation.

† The word used is "*páṭ*". A *páṭ* in Rangpur is the term used for one of those solid blocks of masonry found here and there in the district. Kings of the olden days are said to have sat upon them, and there to have dispensed justice. One of them, however, *(Haris' Chandra Rájár Páṭ,* see fig. 3), is almost certainly a tomb.

and wept. 404. At the *ghát* of the *Ghátwál* there were twenty-two *káhans** of ships, and they all wept. Twenty-two *káhans* of ships wept and twenty-three *káhans* of boatmen, and amongst them Vis'ves'var the boatman also wept. 405. The deer-park wept and the children's summer-house. Even the school of harlots wept. 406. The *Ṭiṭiyá Manjar* wept within its cage. And nine *buḍis*† of dogs wept as they were hunting. 407. The hospital and the *toshá-khána* wept at intervals. Water-houses, summer-houses and cow-houses‡ (?) wept in countless number. 408. In the elephant stalls, the elephants wept. In the stables, the horses wept. In the throne-room, all the dresses were wet with tears. 409. A hundred cows wept, throwing their tails round the king's neck §; and nine *buḍis* of dogs wept at his feet. 410. A hundred queens rolled upon the earth and wept. Aduná and Paduná clasped his feet and wept.

Aduna' and Paduna' spake.

411. "Alas, alas, my husband, my wealth. Thou art deserting me. Who now will protect me, and bring me *ghí* and rice to eat?" 412. The king's mother wept with tears falling from her eyes, and they brought a jar of Gangá water. 413. They brought a leaf of a Newáij tree, and they poured water on him from a golden cup. 414. As they poured water on the head of the king, the royal throne quaked. 415. The barber grasped his razor and gazed around. But he received no order to shave the king.

Mayana' spake.

416. "O barber, towards whom art thou looking? Scorn not thou to shave the head of my darling. Diamonds will I give thee and mounted work; pearls will I give thee as a token. 417. Shave off all his hair, leave only one crown-lock. If thou shavest it off, thereby wilt thou lose thy quilt and wallet." 418. He took his razor in his hand and for a hundred days the king's hair fell upon earth. It became a hairy Gangá and began to flow away. 419. Mayaná uttered "*Tuḍu, Tuḍu*" with a terrible cry, and sixteen hundred *Munis* came down on hearing it. 420. In his chariot of flowers descended Gorakh the Vidyádhara. On a flail came riding Nárada, best of munis. 421. On the back of Vásoyár descended the mighty Bholánáth. On bow and arrow came down Ráma and Lakshmaṇa. 422. In different directions descended the five Páṇḍava brothers. There

* A *káhan* = 16 *pans* of 20 *gaṇḍas* or 1280.

† A *buḍi* = 5 *gaṇḍas* or twenty.

‡ The meaning of *gokula* here is unknown to every one whom I have consulted.

§ I know of no other flight of poetry equal to this in the whole poem. I have tried hard to persuade myself that the translation is incorrect; but in vain. The words are too plain to admit of any other meaning.

is no counting the number of Háḍi *Siddhas*, with their ears cut. 423. A Háḍi hid his face with the dust of cow-dung fuel; and seeing danger at hand, Mayaná began to weep.

THE BURDEN OF HER SONG.

424. "The apple of his mother's eyes. Alas, my child! Who took my own away?" 425. They snatched the razor from the hands of the *nápit*, and gave it into the hand of the ear-cutter. 426. Even as the ear-cutter took the razor in his hand, he cried "*Rám*, *Rám*" and cut both the ears of the king. 427. They fastened to the king's ear an ear-ring of crystal. They clothed him in a cloth covered with holy symbols. 428. Five Vaishṇavas came and dressed the king in a *languṭi*. A *languṭi* with a string did they put upon him. 429. They placed round his neck a *Ráma* rosary. They put into his hand a gourd-platter. 430. A torn quilt, a torn *languṭi*, a torn (heart at) departure. All the followers of Chaitanya were collected near the door. 431. Holy Chaitanya and Nityánanda, also Rádhá, Sítá, and the High Priest of the Vaishṇavas sang the Holy Lay. 432. The king's son began to weep, and cried for alms. His servant Khetu gave him alms: elephants, horses, his royal staff and umbrella. Those alms he placed with reverence at the feet of his *guru*.

THE GURU SPAKE.

433. "Depart, depart, O king, I give to thee a boon. Thou shalt go to the three corners of the earth, but shalt not go to Yama's dwelling-place." 434. As the king turned his head to one side, all the heavenly *Munis* returned to heaven. 435. Mayaná bathed herself in five *loṭas* of water, and glad in heart she entered into her own home. 436. In a moment,* she cooked a dish of rice and fifty curries. She touched it, and placed it in a golden dish. 437. She filled a golden vessel with water. "Eat, eat my darling. Happy and light of heart, go thou on thy pilgrimage." 438. When he saw the rice in a (golden) plate, he struck his forehead with his hand, and wept.

THE KING SPAKE.

439. "When I was lord of my kingdom, O my mother, then did I eat rice in many a golden dish. 440. Now I am a beggar, not worth a single *káoṛi*. I cannot eat from a golden plate." 441. He took a plantain leaf and cut it. Thereon he placed a little rice. 442. He took the shell of a broken gourd and from it he drank a little water. 443. He washed his face and hands with water. Then what did he do? He uttered the words "S'rí Krishṇa" and ate the food. 444. One mouthful, two

* Lit. at a stroke.

mouthfuls, five mouthfuls he ate. Then he looked towards the water, which was trickling out of the broken gourd. 445. He put his face to the earth and sipped up the water, and as he did so Deví's brother S'ani* came over his destiny. 446. S'ani and Ketu took up their abode in the king's heart. And all his body became defiled. 447. Then Mayaná wept in pitiful accents.

THE BURDEN OF HER SONG.

448. "My son is all my fortune. Who will make us meet again. 449. Thou art going to a far country. Thou wilt dwell in the house of a strange woman. First the householder will eat and then he will think of thee. 450. When thou seest an Atíta or a Vaishṇava do not thou despise him. With thy head touching the ground reverence thou him who weareth a rosary. 451. When thou shalt see the mustard plant scanty, and the *dub* grass thin; then wilt thou know that thou art in a far country."

THE KING SPAKE.

452. "If I see a flower, I will not pluck it. If I see a bird, I will not fling a stone at it. 453. If I see another's wife, I will not smile at her. First I will call her mother, then will I ask for alms." 454. She put sixteen *kahans* of *káoṛís* in his wallet. "See that thou tellest not thy guru about these *káoṛís*." 455. "In dust and ashes will I spend the money. Following the Háḍi will I go to Yama's abode."

456. The hundred queens went to Khetu. But Aduná and Paduná went to their own palace. 457. In that palace, there were guards in twelve places, and thirteen *thánás*. No Atíta or Vaishṇava was allowed to enter that house. 458. And e'en as the two damsels entered their dwelling-place, the doors of virtue shut themselves without keys. 459. They set themselves to play at dice in silence.

THE QUEEN SPAKE.

460. "What day the dice will fall from my hands in disorder, I shall know that that day my husband is dead."

461. The burden of the kingdom remained in the lap of Mayaná, the king's mother. And the Háḍi and the king started for a city in a far country. 462. One *kroś*, two *kroś*, five *kroś* he went. And the king's feet were cut and covered with blood.

THE BURDEN OF HIS SONG.

463. "Alas! Fate, sitting in a lovely place, hath written misery on my destiny." 464. One day, two days, seven days passed. Night and

* S'ani and Ketu of course mean ill-luck. If, however, by "Deví" is meant Durgá, she is certainly not S'ani's sister.

day he journeyed on. 465. So the king left his home and went to another country, and the Háḍi said, " Glory to fate. This is the fruit of my destiny."

THE HA'ḌI SPAKE.

466. " A proud word did the king speak concerning me. Verily, in a short space, I will bring him into trouble." 467. " *Tuḍu, Tuḍu,*" cried he, with a terrible voice ; and in the atmosphere that wondrous Háḍi created a forest. 468. They passed through a small forest, and came to a great one. The spittle in the king's mouth was dried up, nor could he speak. 469. In the vacant atmosphere the Háḍi went along. While the king toiled slowly along, thrusting the *jangal* aside with his hands. 470. Prickles pierced him and thorns pierced him. His blood poured forth in streams. He could not travel further, and (in despair) the king struck his forehead with his hand.

THE BURDEN OF HIS SONG.

471. " To whom shall I tell my woes. Even my guru hath become pitiless." 472. More pangs he gave the king. He took him through a sandy waste. At the king's tears the Háḍi's heart was touched, and he created a pleasant Kadamba tree upon the road. 473. The king went to a place deep (under the foliage) by the foot of the tree, and sleep came upon him in handfuls.

THE KING SPAKE.

474. " What with ploughing through water, and what with ploughing through sand, I have undergone great hardships. Place thy left thigh upon the ground, that I may rest awhile. 475. The Háḍi laid his left thigh upon the ground, and the king rested his head upon it and fell asleep. 476. The Háḍi cried " *Tuḍu, Tuḍu*" with a loud voice, and summoned an hundred Yamas.

THE HA'ḌI SPAKE.

477. " Hear, O ye Yamas, take heed unto my words. Build ye a road from hence to Daryápur, seven cubits broad and chest high." 478. The Yamas heard his words, nor did they delay. They departed to build the road. 479. From thence to Daryápur they built the road, seven cubits broad and chest high. 480. " *Hanumán*" he cried with a loud voice, and made them plant trees at intervals along the road. 481. He smote the king with a slap like a thunderbolt, and crying " Guru, Guru" the king arose, weeping.

THE HA'ḌI SPAKE.

482. " I have built a road with great labour. Give me twelve *káoṛís*, that I may buy happiness and enjoy myself. 483. I would buy and eat

twelve *káoṛís* worth of *gánjá:* then will I take thee on to Ghádapur." 484. When the pious king heard these words, he closed his ears, and cried "Rám, Rám."

THE KING SPAKE.

485. "I know nought of such a thing, O father guru. He who goeth with such a transgressor, will surely die. 486. Nay, nay, there is no need of binding me. Instead of twelve *káoṛís* take twelve *káhans*, and return unto thy house." 487. The Háḍi was in contemplation and suddenly started. 488. He went into contemplation and gazed about, and in his contemplation his eyes fell upon the sixteen *káhans* in the king's wallet.

THE HA'ḌI SPAKE.

489. "His mother excelleth me in charms. She hath put sixteen *káhans* of *káoṛís* in his wallet." 490. He cried "*Tuḍu, Tuḍu*" with a loud voice, and took the sixteen *káhans* of *káoṛís*, and flew up into the sky. 491. He created two stones weighing half a *man* each, and put them into the wallet. And the pious king took his *bhát* and began to eat. 492. "Give me, give me the *káoṛís*," he began to coax. But after saying so twice or thrice, he became angry. 493. The king opened the wallet and became amazed. Wonderful thing! No *káoṛís* were within the wallet.

THE BURDEN OF HIS SONG.

494. "Why do my eyes dance in my head? I know not what is written in my fate. 495. Why, why, O father guru, hast thou wrongfully given up pity? In my wallet there are no *káoṛís*. Give me, unhappy one, in pawn for the *káoṛís* I have promised." 496. Immediately the Háḍi called his mother-earth to witness. "I call thee to witness, that he himself hath offered himself in pawn. 'Tis not the Háḍi who hath given him." 497. He put the pious king in his wallet, and took him to the city of Daryápur.

THE HA'ḌI SPAKE.

498. "A man for pawn, a man for pawn. Take him, O mother, thou seller of milk. I would pawn him for twelve *káoṛís*. I wish to get twelve *káoṛís* to eat *gánjá*."

THE GOWÁLINÍ SPAKE.

499. "See, see, we would see what kind of pupil this is of thine." 500. He pulled the king out by one hand, and the king arose radiant in person.

THE GOWÁLINÍ SPAKE.

501. "I perceive that he is of beautiful form and accustomed to eat royal food.* Can such as he eat in the house of a Gowáliní? 502. Fill up my milk-pail with money, and fill up thy wallet again. Leave my quarter of the town, and go thou elsewhere." 503. He seized the king by the hand, and wandered about amongst the shop lanes. 504. "A man for pawn, a man for pawn, O mother, thou seller of crushed rice" and as soon as the crushed rice-seller saw the king, she upset her stall of crushed rice. 505. She clasped him round the waist, saying, "I die (of love for thee)"; and with great difficulty the king separated himself from her. 506. "A man for pawn, a man for pawn, O mother, thou seller of turmeric. A man for pawn, a man for pawn, O mother, thou seller of *ság*. 507. A man for pawn, a man for pawn, O mother, thou seller of vetch. A man for pawn, a man for pawn, O mother, thou seller of pease." 508. And as soon as the seller of pease saw the king, she immediately called her own husband her father. 509. She upset her stall; she caught the king by the waist exclaiming "I die." 510. The crushed rice-seller arose and said to the pease-seller "You get away. Let go the waist of the king. I first caught hold of him." 511. They both caught him by the waist and began to pull; and of a sudden the king began to weep. 512. The Háḍi felt pity at the tears of the king, and called on Indra with a loud cry. 513. With great noise, hail began to fall in the *bazár*. And they let go the king's waist, and every one went to her house. 514. "Don't stop up the door, don't stop up the door, O sister, seller of pease. Don't you see that I'll catch my death out here in the wet"? 515. And when the seller of pease heard that word, she made a great fuss, and left the door free for passengers. 516. The Háḍi took the pestle for pounding pease, and with it began to pound the king. 517. He cut the king's nose, and his hair, and made proclamation by beat of drum. He put his hand upon the king's neck, and pushed him out from that *bazár*. 518. He left that locality, and went to Vijaya the ploughman, and stopped before him. 519. "A man for pawn, a man for pawn, O house of a *halwá*." 520. "Outwardly† he is of comely form. How can he eat in the house of a ploughman? 521. Fit for him is the house of Hírá, the harlot; but how wilt thou go within her house? 522. She hath hung a pair of drums by her door, and if the king of any quarter come to her abode, 523. And if he strike the drum one blow, she will demand a thousand rupees at the door." 524. Vijaya went away with them, and showed them the harlot's house. 525. He took down the stick and smote the drum, and by its sound his arrival was made known in the house of the harlot. 526. She

* Lit. "a king over his *bhát*."   † Lit. over the vessel.

began to call to her maid-servant. "The king of what country has now come? Allow him to enter, and fan him with a *chámara.*" 527. The maid-servant heard her, nor did she delay, but went into the presence of the Háḍi.

THE MAID-SERVANT SPAKE.

528. "Why, Reverend Sir, hast thou come so far a distance? Why hast thou left thy throne, to lie upon the earth?"

THE HA'ḌI SPAKE.

529. "It is not bamboo oil vessels, nor *bazár* cups that I carry in my wallet. Herein have I a pupil. 530. I would pawn him for twelve *káoṛís*, to buy *gánjá* that I may eat. 531. Will Hirá, the harlot, take him in pledge?"

THE MAID-SERVANT SPAKE.

"Let me see, let me see what sort of pupil he is." 532. He pulled him forth by one hand, and the king arose radiant in person.

THE BURDEN OF HER SONG.

533. "On seeing his beauty, my eyes run with tears." 534. The maid-servant told the harlot what she had heard. "The king is more beautiful in his feet than thou art in thy face. 535. The king for whom thou hast been offering sacrifices these twelve years; him thou hast found at thy very door." 536. On hearing this, the harlot did not delay, but went before the king.

THE HA'ḌI SPAKE.

537. "Hear, oh harlot, what I have to say unto thee. A good pupil is this whom I would pledge with thee. 538. I would pledge him for twelve *káoṛís*, that with them I may buy *gánjá*." 539. On hearing this, the harlot did not delay, but sent to the *bazár* for a *sáud* banker. 540. She collected the paper and pens and counted out twelve *káoṛís*. 541. In a clear voice, the Háḍi told the banker to write, and he wrote the year, the date, and the word *S'rí* on the paper. 542. He wrote the name of Hírá, the harlot, on the paper and also the twelve *káoṛís*. 543. He wrote the name of Dharma on the paper, and threw the pen to the Háḍi. 544. And when that mighty Háḍi took the pen in his hand, he uttered the words "Rám, Rám" and made his signature. 545. She counted out the twelve *káoṛís* and gave them to the Háḍi, who on his part made over the king to the harlot. 546. And from the day that the Háḍi gave the deed into the harlot's hand, the king lay pawned with her. 547. The Muni Háḍi tightly tied up the passions of the king and made him neither a woman nor a man. 548. When Hírá, the harlot, turned her head to one side, he

buried the twelve *káorís* in the earth. 549. And when the pious king turned his face away, he turned himself into a golden pumpkin and went to the regions of Pátála. 550. Beneath fourteen fathoms of water he took his magic seat, and for twelve years he stayed there in contemplation. 551. When the king turned round again, and could no longer see his Guru, he began to weep.

The Harlot spake.

552. "O king, why dost thou weep? For thy sake I have been doing penance these twelve years. 553. Where art thou gone, my maid-servant? Bring me *pán* to eat* and then bathe the king, and make him put on all the radiancy he can." 554. The maid-servant brought the king after bathing him. The harlot well knew how to spread a bed. 555. Over a coarse mat she spread fine mats as high as the chest, and over all she laid an *indra-kambal*.† 556. She made ready cloves, nutmegs and camphor for eating: so much, that there would be no counting the number of times the king would spit. 557. As soon as the pious king entered into the room, she took him in her lap, and sat him on the bed, and offered him a vessel of *pán*. 558. "Eat a *khili*‡ of *pán*, and eat a single betel-nut, O king. Lift up thy head and gaze upon this luckless harlot." 559. The king was pleased in his heart when he saw the cloves, nutmegs and camphor, and at one time she gave him four or five *khilis*. 560. Once, twice, and thrice he bruised the *khili* in his fingers, and then the warning of his mother came into his remembrance. 561. "Thou art going to a far country. Thou wilt dwell in the house of a strange woman. First the householder will eat, and then he will think of thee. 562. When thou seest an Atíta or a Vaishṇava do not thou despise him. With thy head touching the ground, reverence thou him who weareth a rosary. 563. If thou seest a flower, thou shalt not pluck it. If thou seest a bird, thou shalt not break its eggs. 564. If thou seest another's wife, thou shalt not smile at her. 565. When thou shalt see the mustard plant scanty, and the *dub* grass thin, then wilt thou know that thou art in a far country." 566. When the words of his mother came into his mind, the king cried, "Rám, Rám," and flung the *khili* of *pán* away. 567. Thereupon the harlot became angry, "Why, O king of kings, dost thou not eat the *pán?* For thy sake I have been doing penance these twelve years." 568. She took five *khilis* in her own hand, and put them in the pious king's mouth, but he cast them out, saying "*thu, thu.*" 569. As the king moved

* See note to v. 373.

† A kind of blanket.

‡ See note to v. 53.

from place to place and sat down, the harlot followed him and sat close up to his body. 570. She began to scatter white and red sandal-wood over his body, but the king began to call her "Mother, mother", and she replied "My heart doth not let me, O king, be called 'mother' by thee." 571. The harlot placed the king's hand upon her heart, but he called her mother, and asked her to suckle him. 572. Once, twice, and thrice the king became angered. He even three or four times abused the harlot.

THE BURDEN OF HIS SONG.

573. "I tell thee the words of thy heart. Unholy is such love. Vainly hast thou lit thy wax candle, and passed a waking night. I am blessed by Ráma; and Kubujá was not (loved by Krishṇa) as Rádhá was. 574. A harlot hath no loveliness within her, her beauty is nought but copious locks of hair. She is but a gift fit for a barber, like the *dhaturá** flower. 575. I see a harlot's dealings to be like a ferry-boat. Men pay *káoṛís* at the landing-stage, and pass over. 576. I see thee, O harlot, to be like traffic in things of no value. Thy beauty is like that of a dark well. Low caste *háḍis* and *doms* as well as bráhmaṇs, bathe (to wash off the defilement) after touching thee." 577. For four watches, the harlot argued, but still the pious king addressed her as "Mother." 578. Once, twice, and thrice did the harlot become angry, at last she kicked the pious king off the bedstead. 579. She called for her maid-servant, who turned the king out with her hand on his neck. 580. The harlot's dress was a linen *sári* bright as fire; but the king's became a knotted rope. 581. Unsifted rice and brinjals full of seeds she gave him; brinjals full of seeds, and he burned them, and made chutney of them. A pitiless harlot was she; she forbade him salt and oil. 582. In the cold month of Mágh, she gave him an old tattered *sári*, and a goat hut to live in. 583. *Bhángi* ropes she gave him, and a *bhángi* stick, and two water-jars. Twelve loads of water did he measure out the livelong day. 584. If one amongst the twelve was not supplied, in payment for it seven men would beat him. 585. He took *bhángi* ropes and a *bhángi* stick and two vessels of water; and he went to fill them at the Karátoyá river. 586. One, two, or three loads he filled. The whole day the Mahárája was carrying the twelve loads. 587. Seven vile men seized the king and laid him on his back and then the harlot would put on her feet golden pattens. 588. Hírá, the harlot, after bathing would laugh gleefully, and proudly stand upon the king's chest. 589. After bathing her body, she shone with excessive brilliancy, and she took off her wet clothes, and put on a dry linen *sári*. 590. The wet clothes she would wring out over the king's face. At midday the king would cover his face and

* Fair to look upon, but has no scent.

weep. She then would seize him by the neck and thrust him out. 591. What with to-day and what with to-morrow twelve years passed. 592. He took *bhángi* ropes and a *bhángi* stick and two water-jars, and went to draw water at the river Karátoyá. 593. On the bank of the river, the king became giddy and fell into the river. "Alas! I heard not the words of Aduná and Paduná, and have lost my life through attending to the voice of an old mother."

594. Even as the pious king mentioned the names of the damsels, the dice fell from their hands in disarray. And lamentably they began to weep. 595. "Twelve years have passed and my husband doth not let his voice be heard, and now the thirteenth year has come. 596. To-day why have the dice fallen in disorder? Of a surety my husband is dead and gone."

THE BURDEN OF HER SONG.

597. "My love, how may I go forth? To-morrow at dawn and in a lonely place will I tell thee the tale of my woes. He playeth his pipe in Vṛindávana: and my heart saith unto me, let me go and see Kṛishṇa." 598. The two sisters went out to the theatrum of the temple in tears. And a jay and a parrot from their cage heard them weeping.

THE JAY SPAKE.

599. "O parrot, my elder brother, let us see why our mother weepeth." 600. They united their strength and burst the bars of their cage, and through the broken walls they flew away. 601. After resting* for a moment on the straw of the thatch, they each alighted on the arm of the damsels. "Why, why, mother, art thou crying in the theatrum?" 602. Ths damsel said, "Listen to me, ye two dear birds. Your father should have returned according to his agreement after twelve years. It is now the thirteenth year and he hath not come. 603. Why did the dice fall in disorder from our hands? Of a surety I believe that your father is dead and gone." 604. "Mother, let us two loose. We will search where our father is." 605. "Speed ye, speed ye, my pretty children, to a far country, and find out where your father is." 606. The birds made obeisance at the feet of their mistress, and flew away in a southern direction. 607. For seven days the birds flew, but found no trace of the king. 608. On the banks of the river there were a banyan and a píppal tree, and the birds flew and rested on a branch of the banyan tree. 609. The birds flew from the western branch to the eastern branch, and underneath them passed the king bearing his burden. 610. He descended into the water and cleansed his teeth, and over his head the birds began to hover.

* Lit. Scratching.

The birds spake.

611. "Art thou the king Gopí Chandra? We two brothers have come for news of thee." 612. He stretched forth his arm, and the two birds settled down upon it. 613. The eyes of the king flowed with affection, as he commenced the tale of his woes. 614. He plucked the leaves of some wild plants (that grew by), and with his teeth he mended a reed pen. 615. He cut his left thigh with his little finger, and wrote a letter with the blood. All his woes he wrote within it. 616. "If thou art a good mother, thou wilt rescue me. If thou art a bad mother, thou wilt leave me in sin." "This letter give ye to your grandmother." 617. The birds made obeisance to the king and flew off to Mayaná's abode. 618. They made a hole in the roof and threw in the letter "See, see, oh Grandam, see if thy head* is in this? 619. If thou art a good mother thou wilt rescue him." 620. She opened the envelope and began to read: and lamentably the birds began to weep.

The burden of her song.

621. "My son left me in the morning. I fear that he hath died in the fierce heat of the sun." 622. Mayaná went into contemplation and gazed around, and her eyes fell upon the Háḍi sitting beneath fourteen fathoms of water. 623. She brought into play her magic art called *kharupá* (or cutting), and she cut away the Háḍi's seat of contemplation and himself. 624. He began to float away through the cold sea; but Mayaná seized him by the hair and pulled him on land. 625. She struck him a slap forcible as a thunderbolt; and the Háḍi who was still in contemplation got up with a start. 626. In his contemplation the Háḍi gazed around, and his eyes fell upon Mayaná. 627. "O sister, I am going to the king. I will first rescue thy son, and then will I eat my *gánjá*.

Mayana' spake.

628. "If I find that my son hath learned only a few charms, I will burn thee, O Háḍi, to ashes, and send thee to Yama's house." 629. The Háḍi started, and arrived at the *ghát* where the king was sitting. 630. As soon as the king saw the Háḍi's face, he laid down the two water-jars and broke them. 631. He divided his hair in the middle and fell at the feet of the Háḍi. 632. Thereupon the Háḍi put him into his wallet and carried him off to the harlot's house. 633. When he arrived there, he uttered a loud cry, and the whole city began to quake with a rumbling noise. 634. The harlot said to her maid-servant "Daughter, see who it be. If it be a beggar, send him away." 635. The maid-servant hastened to the door and when she saw the Háḍi she returned to her mistress. 636.

* *i. e.*, if this concerneth thee.

She said unto the harlot, "It is not an Atíta, but the Háḍi the lord of Lanka." 637. When the harlot heard this, what did she do? She went inside the house and hid herself. 638. The harlot said to herself "I am hidden." But the mighty Háḍi saw her by his power of contemplation, and grasped his staff. 639. "I tell thee my staff, and pay thou heed unto my words. Bind Hírá, the harlot, and bring her forth." 640. The staff received one order as if it were a thousand, and with a roar it entered the harlot's house. 641. It thrust the harlot forth, and then the Háḍi took up the twelve *káoṛís*. 642. The harlot brought forth the deed executed twelve years ago, and he counted into her hands the twelve *káoṛís*. 643. She gave the deed into his hand, and the Háḍi said, "Rám, Rám," as he tore it up. 644. The Háḍi brought a cauldron of Ganges water, and seven vile men seized the harlot and threw her on her back. 645. He put on the king's foot pattens weighing twenty-two maunds, and stood the king upon the harlot's breast. 646. As he swayed upon her in mounting, he crushed the harlot's thirty-two ribs into small pieces. 647. As soon as the Háḍi sprinkled water on the king's head, saying "Rám, Rám," all his sin was put away from him. 648. After bathing his body, he shone with excessive brightness, and he took off his wet clothes and put on a dry linen *dhuṭi*.

The Há'ḍi spake.

649. "O prince, pay heed unto my words. For twelve years the harlot hath done penance in her house. Do thou fulfil to some extent her desires. 650. Go forth, O Hírá the harlot, I give to thee a boon. Become a bat within the kingdom." 651. The Muni's word was not spoken in vain: she became a bat, and flew up to heaven. 652. He caught hold of the harlot in his left hand, and divided her into two parts. 653. The forepart flew up to heaven, but he cast the rear-part into the sea. 654. As she fell into the sea she cried "*doház*."

The Há'ḍi spake.

655. "Go forth, O Hírá, thou harlot, I give to thee a boon. Become a minnow, and dwell within the water. 656. Go forth, go forth, O Chápái, thou maid-servant, I give to thee a boon. Become a harlot, and live within the kingdom. 657. In thy youth earn thy living out of the work of thy caste; and in thy old age, take a *páik* for thy husband. He will beat thee and kick thee and break thy thirty-two ribs. 658. Go forth, O wealth of Hírá, I give to thee a boon. Come into the town of Kholáháṭi, and be a petty *bazár* made of tiles." 659. He utterly destroyed Hírá's house, and then took the king away to teach him magic arts.

THE HA'ḌI SPAKE.

660. "I say unto thee, O king, and take thou heed unto my words. Go thou into the market and beg for alms. Let us sit together, as *guru* and disciple, in the town of Pardá."

THE KING SPAKE.

661. "I am a king's son, and have become a Brahmáchárí. How can I beg? I know not how to do it." 662. So the Háḍi gave him three or four directions, and the king took a platter in his hand and went to beg.

THE HA'ḌI SPAKE.

663. "Victory to fate, this is the fruit of my works. I have in my house a pupil, beautiful in every limb. He will drive the daughters-in-law and the daughters of the householders mad. 664. He changed himself into Nengaḍi the *Koṭwál* and went about fastening the door bars in every house. 665. He is bending forward entreating for alms, and they are setting the dogs at him. He will not get any alms, and will return to the Háḍi." 666. The king went about begging, but the Háḍi cried out with a loud voice. 667. And from heaven there came down at his call five damsels, who placed five dishes of food before him. 668. He ate his own share, and put aside that of the king with care, and in it he put two and a half times sixteen scores of charms. 669. He mixed it with spittle and phlegm, and added to it the juice of refined* sugar. *Sáil* seeds, *kelá* seeds and *durá* seeds he added to the mess. 670. Meanwhile the pious king went about crying for alms. 671. He bent forward entreating for alms, and they set dogs at him. He was unsuccessful in his quest, and returned to the presence of the Háḍi.

THE KING SPAKE.

672. "O guru, the people of thy country I have seen to be pitiless and stony-hearted. They gave neither alms nor charity, and set the dogs at me."

THE HA'ḌI SPAKE.

673. "Thou hast not obtained alms. It mattereth not, my son. Accept the leavings of my food. I met a pious woman on the road. 674. She gave me a little rice. I have eaten my share, and carefully put some aside for thee." 675. With tottering steps the king drew near the food. And when he saw it he struck his forehead with his hand. 676. A rice which my dogs would turn aside from; such have I, a king, come to eat. 677. "*Tuḍu, Tuḍu,*" said the Háḍi with a great voice; and the king felt an-hungered as if he had fasted for twelve years. 678. He took

* Lit. covered.

his first mouthful with expressions of disgust, but it came to his taste like sweet ambrosia. 679. When again he put forth his hand to take a mouthful, he snatched at it, thrusting aside the Háḍi's hand, and took two and a half mouthfuls at once. And therefrom he learnt two and a half times sixteeen scores of charms. 680. By his charms in his meditation he bound up his top-knot as a woman ties it, and embraced the mother of Godá Yama. 681. By his charms, in his meditation, he tied up his top-knot as a man ties it, and lamed Godá Yama himself. 682. The Háḍi uttered the words "*Tuḍu, Tuḍu*" with a loud voice and thereupon the affairs of his home came in the king's remembrance.

THE KING SPAKE.

683. "Give me leave, O guru, and let me journey forth in the bark of virtue. Travelling in a chariot of light, would I see my wife and home, and then return to thee." 684. He placed his staff in the hands of the king, who thereupon fell at the feet of the Háḍi. 685. The king carried the stick over his shoulder (although it weighed) eighty maunds; and started off for his own home. 686. The mighty Háḍi laughed aloud, and the king left him and started on his journey. 687. He reached his palace, and cried "*Tuḍu, Tuḍu*" with a roar like a lion. The damsels were asleep but now awoke. 688. Without being struck, the gongs at the gate sounded; and without fire being applied, milk and rice began to boil. 689. In all the little *bazárs* the lamps began to blaze. The king began to float in a sea of delight.* 690. A swarm of bees flew up around his head. The king saw the delights of holy Vṛindávana before his eyes. And all pregnant women gave birth to their offsprings.

THE QUEEN SPAKE.

THE BURDEN OF HER SONG.

691. "A pilgrim hath come, and standeth in my door. 692. Where is the maid-servant. I would first eat *pán*,† and then (would I enquire) whence the pilgrim hath come, and dismiss him." 693. The maid-servant made ready alms. 694. "Take alms, O reverend pilgrim, I am the maid of a householder, and would return within the house."

THE KING SPAKE.

695. "I am a pilgrim from the south: I call myself a Brahmáchárí. I cannot take alms from the humble hands of a maid-servant. 696. If a lady give me alms, then this pilgrim's son can take it."

* Lit. coldness.

† See note to v. 373.

THE MAID-SERVANT SPAKE.

697. "Wait awhile, O pilgrim, thou who sittest and beggest shamelessly. Long will it be before thou obtainest alms, even though thou criest for them." 698. The maid-servant went weeping to the damsel. "He is a pilgrim from the south, and calleth himself Brahmáchárí. 699. He taketh not alms from the hands of a maid-servant, but saith, 'Let the ladies give me alms.'" 700. When the two damsels heard this they took alms and arose. Behold, without a key the door opened of itself. 701. Aduná and Paduná went out with the alms. "Take alms, take alms, O reverend pilgrim. We are the daughters-in-law of a householder, and would return within the house."

THE KING SPAKE.

702. "I am a pilgrim from the east. My name is Brahmáchárí. I cannot take alms from the hand of a woman. 703. If the umbrella* that shadeth thy head can give me alms, then can this pilgrim's son accept them." 704. The ladies pointed out the ring upon his finger. "We see a woman's ring upon thy hand. 705. Thou art the umbrella of my head. Thou art a pilgrim, and I am a pilgrim, pupils of one guru."

THE KING SPAKE.

706. "One evening I stopped at a house, and they gave to a man *ṭhákari kálái ḍál* and *áuś* rice. 707. He ate it greedily, and was attacked with cholera and died. 708. First one man took something† off his body, and then another; and as my share they gave me these two rings."

THE QUEEN SPAKE.

709. "Where is my maid-servant? First will she eat *pán*.‡ Then shall she cut the rope which ties the elephant. 710. If this be my husband, he will recognize him. If he be a pilgrim from the south, he will trample him to death." 711. She cut the elephant's rope, and the elephant came from a distance. 712. While yet afar off he made obeisance to the king. And when he approached, he lifted him on to his shoulder with his trunk. 713. The elephant awaited awhile and stood steady, that the damsels might approach. 714. The king descended from the back of the elephant, and the damsels took him by the hand and led him within the house. Amid laughter and jokes, they began to speak familiarly with him.

* *I. e.*, thy husband.

† So explained to me. It means literally, "First one gave a blow, and then another gave the last blow."

‡ See note to v. 373.

The Queen spake.

715. "How hath the Guru taught thee magic arts? Let us see how thou wilt approach thy mother." 716. He changed himself into a golden bee, and flew to his mother's palace. 717. He appeared in Mayaná's house, and, uttering a loud cry, made her spinning-wheel fly up into the air. 718. But Mayaná also was skilled in charms, and with a jump she seized the spinning-wheel by its head.

Mayana' spake.

719. "Come, come my son, the darling of an unhappy one." 720. The king divided his hair and fell at the feet of his mother. 721. He sent for Mathu the barber. He began to clear off his vow,* and the Bráhmaṇs came, and collected materials for sacrifice. 722. The king began to perform the celebration of the office of *sankírttana* and gave away the contents of seven barns in charity. 723.† He himself crossed the Vaitaraṇi on the tail of a cow, and his ancestors crossed (the river of life) into paradise. 724. Mayaná bathed herself with five *loṭas* of water, and laughing returned quickly‡ into the house. 725. After cooking a dish of rice and fifty different curries, she cleaned three (brass plates) with tamarind juice. 726. Mayaná summoned the Háḍi with a loud voice, and he immediately came and stood before her. 277. The first plate she gave to the Háḍi. The second she took herself, and the third she gave to the king. 728. After washing their hands and mouth, what did they do? They uttered the holy name of Kṛishṇa, and, beginning their meal, ate one, two, and five mouthfuls each. 729. After eating and drinking, their hearts were glad, and they washed their mouths with water from a golden vessel. 730. Then the Háḍi, who came from paradise, placed his feet on the head of the king, and returned to his own place. 731. They cleaned the king's throne; and Hanumán took the staff and umbrella of royalty, and marched about; and the throne-elephant approached dressed in his trappings. 732. The king clothed himself magnificently, and the elephant mounted him on his shoulders by his trunk. 733. He took the king to the throne, accompanied by the music of drums and trumpets; and bowed himself down before it, and with his trunk placed him upon the seat. 734. Then the king immediately fixed the land revenue at one and a half scores of *káoṛís*, (as it had been in old days) and ever since reigned happily within his kingdom.

* By cutting his nails and hair which he had allowed to grow.

† This is most essentially a "*Satya yuger kathá.*" What *does* it mean?

‡ Lit. At a bound.

APPENDIX.

The following are the lines referred to in the note to verse 264. I give them as an example of the very peculiar nature of the dialect. It is difficult, and requires a very literal translation, which I give.

The word for "fresh butter" appears in two forms,—ननि and नवनि ; and it is worth noting how the latter has remained almost unchanged from the time of the *Aitareya Bráhmaṇa.**

श्यामर वांशीरे मन मजालुरे ।
रया २ नयान भोरे ॥
माय़ वलेरे याडु उत्तरे ।
गभिन पुष्पर पालङ्क ।
पेय़्रे पार कत निन्द ॥
मायर वचने याडु उठिया वसिल ।
मेलिते ना पारे आंखि घसिते लागिल ॥
याडु गेल छिनाने यश्नदा रल घरे ।
एखिन† नवनि वाटे घरे २ ॥
छिनान करिया घरे नागि याय़ ।
उत्तम सिङ्गसन वसिते दिल माय़ ।
आनन्दित हया याडु खिर ननि खाय़ ॥
खिर ननि खाया याडु तुष्ट हलो मन ।
उत्तम भिङ्गार जले करे आश्रवन‡ ॥

O the pipe of S'yám (Kṛishṇa). My mind whirls, my eyes continually run with tears. The mother said "O Yádu, how art thou sleeping on the deep bed of flowers in the north?" Hearing the mother's voice, Yádu sat up; he could not open his eyes, and began to rub them. Yádu goes to bathe; Yasódá remains in the house, and divides out this rice-milk and fresh butter.

After finishing his bath, he goes towards the house—his mother gives him a grand throne to sit upon; being pleased, Yádu eats the milk, and the fresh butter.

After eating the milk and fresh butter, Yádu's mind becomes satisfied; and he washes his mouth with water in a grand golden pot.

* Ait. Br. I. 3. नवनीतेनाभ्यञ्जन्ति ॥

† एखिन = ए खिर ॥ ‡ आश्रवन = आचमन ॥

SUPPOSED TO REPRESENT VASU DEVA.
SON OF MÁNICK CHANDRA. Fig. 2.

Fig: 3.

Haris Chandra Raja's Tomb.

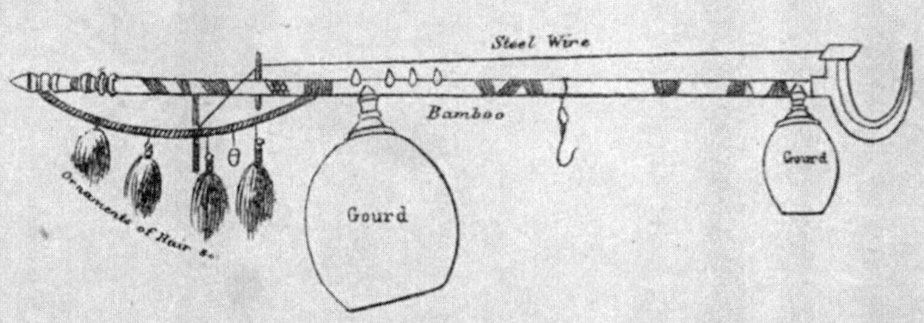

Fig: 4

Saringa or Tambúrá.

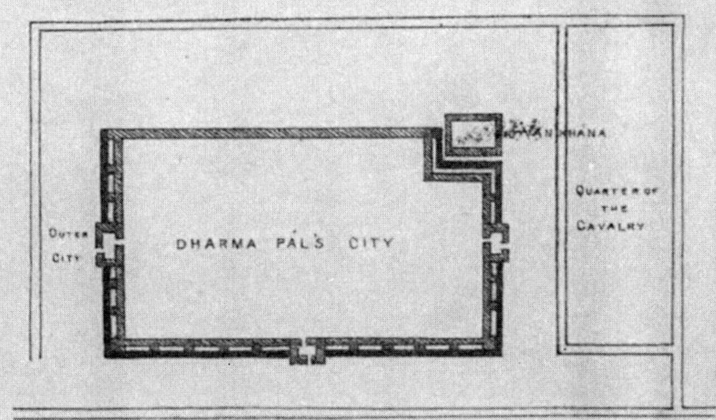

Fig: 1